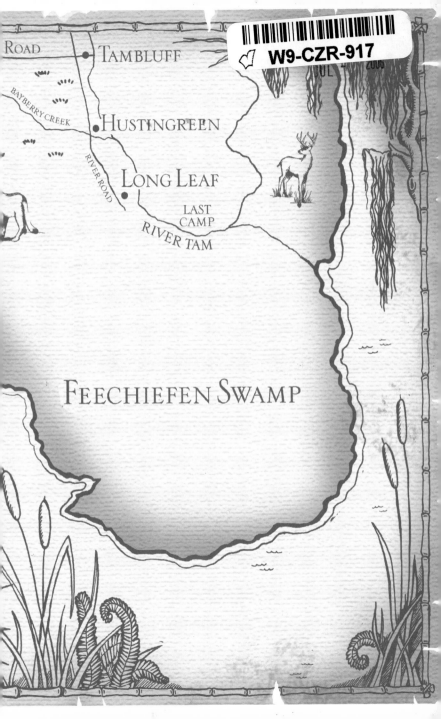

The Secret of the Swamp King

THE WILDERKING TRILOGY

BOOK 2

The Secret of the Swamp King

FEECHIEFEN

JONATHAN ROGERS

BROADMAN
&HOLMAN
PUBLISHERS

NASHVILLE, TENNESSEE

13-digit ISBN: 978-0-8054-3132-2
10-digit ISBN: 0-8054-3132-2

Published by Broadman & Holman Publishers,
Nashville, Tennessee

Dewey Decimal Classification: F
Subject Headings: ADVENTURE FICTION
                   ADOLESCENCE—FICTION

Interior illustrations by Greg Pope
Map by Kristi Smith and Greg Pope

1 2 3 4 5 6 7 8 9 10 09 08 07 06 05

For Heyward, Henry, Lawrence,
Margaret, William, and Betsy,

the original wee-feechies

Chapter One
Canebrake

He's making for the canebrake!" Aidan shouted over the thunder of horses' hooves. Both he and Prince Steren heaved their spears, but the quarry was too far away. The great boar hog slashed his way between wrist-thick stalks of river cane, and his black, bristling mass vanished into the blackness of the canebrake.

Aidan and Steren reined up at the verge of the thicket and pulled their spears out of the spongy ground. "I'll drive him through the cane on the Bear Trail," said Aidan. He knew he had no chance of spearing the boar amid the close-set cane stalks, especially without the boar dogs. But if he could drive the big hog through the brake to the trail along the river's edge, they might get him yet. Aidan gestured toward the south with his spearpoint. "You circle around the canebrake," he ordered, "and come back up the River Trail. I'll try to steer him right into you."

Steren clucked once to his hunting horse and bolted down the edge of the canebrake. Steren was crown prince of Corenwald, the only son of King Darrow. But there was no question about it: When he and Aidan were in the forest, Aidan was in charge.

Aidan nudged his own horse, and they plunged into the narrow gap where the boar had entered the canebrake. Horse and rider crashed down the twisting trail that bears and wildcats used to cut through the vast canebrake to the River Tam. It seemed more tunnel than trail. On either side, cane stalks stood just inches apart, and a foot or so above Aidan's head, their leafy tops closed together in a thick canopy that filtered most of the morning sunlight.

Leaves and wiry branches slapped at Aidan's face on either side as he followed the sound of the boar hog's grunts and the pounding of his sharp hooves. A ropy spider web, stretching across the trail like a birder's net, enfolded Aidan's head and neck in a sticky gauze. He plucked the meaty spider from his hair, wiped his eyes and mouth free of spider web, and kept charging, driving the hog to the other side of the thicket.

Aidan wasn't far behind his quarry. He was close enough to hear the hog but not close enough to see him. Hard though he pressed the chase, he didn't actually want to catch the hog—at least not in the depths of the canebrake. He hardly had room to turn around, much less maneuver a long hunting spear. The hog, on the other hand, was cut out for that kind of close work. He would have more than enough room to use his curving, finger-length tusks to vicious effect.

If the boar had realized he was being pursued by a single fifteen-year-old boy, surely he would have turned and showed tusk rather than tail. But Aidan used a trick he learned from old Lord Cuthbert to make sure he sounded like more than a single hunter. He dragged the butt of his spear along the bamboo stalks as he galloped down the trail, setting up a clatter that sounded like a hundred hunters storming through the brake.

Aidan added to the confusion with a series of feechie battle yells: *"Haaa-wwwweeeeee! Haaa-wwwweeeeee! Haaa-wwwweeeeee!"*

The boar never slowed and never looked back at his pursuer. Terrified by the sounds of the pursuit, he was running harder than ever when he burst out of the canebrake and into the clearing of the River Trail. Aidan's horse emerged twenty strides behind, just in time to see the boar's black rump disappear around the first bend to the north. Prince Steren was nowhere to be seen; he hadn't had nearly enough time to make the wide circuit around the canebrake. And he would be coming from the south. Aidan had not succeeded in driving the hog in Steren's direction the way he had hoped. He clucked to his hard-breathing horse and directed it northward, upstream, in the slim hope that he might be able to overtake the hog before he disappeared into the swamp.

But just as the horse began to lunge forward, a shadow dropped from the limbs of the water oak above Aidan's head. Aidan felt his horse shudder as something lit on its haunches, just behind the saddle skirt. Aidan felt a clammy hand on the nape of his neck, another on his shoulder. The hairs on Aidan's neck prickled at the hot, swampy breath of his attacker. Shocked and frightened, Aidan instinctively swung his elbows behind him, first one then the other, in an effort to knock the shadowy figure to the ground. But the attacker was as agile as a squirrel and easily jumped clear of Aidan's swinging elbows.

Meanwhile, the terrified horse wheeled and bucked to shake free of this second rider. Aidan flew from the saddle and into the sparkleberry bushes that lined the trail. He scrambled for his spear, ducking away from the flying hooves of the horse, which still cavorted and kicked in panic. Aidan backed away to safety and crouched defensively with his hunting spear outthrust.

His attacker, Aidan could now see, was a bare-chested he–feechie, more or less full-grown, in a snakeskin kilt and tortoiseshell helmet. He was doing a ridiculous loose-limbed jig on the horse's back, while it reared, bucked, and whirled. Even when the horse threw the gray-skinned feechie into the air, he somehow managed to regain his footing on the horse's back. The poor horse had a better chance of bucking off a tick.

Then the feechie leaped from the saddle horn, turned a perfect flip, and landed flat-footed in the sand just a stride or two from Aidan's spearpoint.

"Is that how a civilizer howdies an old friend?" asked the feechie, pushing back his helmet and breaking into a greenish, gap-toothed grin. "Poking a cold-shiny jobber stick right in his face?"

Overjoyed, Aidan dropped his spear and opened his arms wide to receive his long-lost friend. "Dobro Turtlebane!" he shouted. "I'd know that smell anywhere!"

Dobro stepped forward as if to embrace Aidan, but he head-butted him instead, then flipped him over his shoulder onto the sandy trail. Dobro pounced on Aidan, meaning to pin him. But the cooks at Tambluff Castle had fed Aidan well in the three years since Dobro had last seen him, and the civilizer had grown strong and big. He easily threw the wiry feechie clear into the bushes.

Rubbing his forehead but grinning nevertheless, Aidan got up to hoist Dobro out of the bushes. But Dobro was nowhere to be found. He had done his old feechie trick. He disappeared, just as he had disappeared three years earlier after they killed the panther in the bottom pasture.

"Dobro!" shouted Aidan. "Dobro! Where have you gotten off to?" But there was no answer. Aidan poked in the bushes with his foot but with no success. Perplexed, he wandered back into the trail to get a wider view.

That's when Dobro dropped from an overhanging tree limb onto Aidan's back. He gripped Aidan in a bear-like headlock. "This here's how feechiefolks says howdy," Dobro laughed.

Aidan's head felt as if it would burst, but he couldn't help laughing, too, from joy and surprise at this un-expected reunion with Dobro. He soon realized he would never pry Dobro's sinewy arms loose, so he dropped onto his back, flattening the scrappy feechie under him. That loosened Dobro's grip just enough for Aidan to escape, and the two friendly combatants rolled on the sandy trail, each trying to pin the other.

Aidan and Dobro were so focused on their rough reunion that they didn't pay attention when Prince Steren reined up beside them and leaped from his horse, spear flashing. Steren was fiercely loyal to Aidan, his best friend in the world. He would never stand idly by and watch Aidan fight off an attack by this . . . this . . . gray-skinned monster or whatever it was.

Steren pointed his spear at the twisting, struggling mass. "Cease!" he shouted, trying to sound as royal and commanding as he could. Startled and still locked in a clench, Aidan and Dobro looked up. Steren brought the spearpoint closer to Dobro. He trembled a little at the fierce glint in the feechie's eye, but he spoke bravely. "I don't know who you are—or what you are. But if you don't unhand my friend, I'll stick this spearpoint right between your ribs."

Dobro sighed in disgust at his own negligence. He could kick himself for letting another civilizer see him. If his mama found out about this, he'd be in deep trouble again. He did as Steren commanded and removed his hands from around Aidan's neck, fixing the prince with a piercing, almost hypnotic glare.

Then, before Steren knew what was happening, Dobro's left hand darted out like a striking rattlesnake and grabbed the spear shaft. With a quick twisting motion he wrenched the spear from Steren's hands, whirled it in a wide-looping circle, and thumped the prince on the head with the butt of the handle. Steren staggered back a step, more astonished than hurt by Dobro's feat of strength and agility.

"You civilizers is the stick-jobbinest bunch I ever seen," observed Dobro. "It ain't good manners." He ran a finger along the steel spearhead. "You could hurt somebody with this cold-shiny thing."

Aidan was laughing now. "Who'd have thought the crown prince of Corenwald would get a lesson in courtesy from a feechie? Steren, meet Dobro Turtlebane. Dobro, this is Steren Darrowson, son of the king."

For a moment, Steren had gone surly, annoyed at Aidan for laughing at him after he had so bravely intervened on his behalf. But at the mention of the word *feechie,* he stared bug-eyed at Dobro as if he were seeing an elf or a unicorn.

"Well, I reckon any friend of Aidan's is my friend," said Dobro, "whatever his manners is like."

He stepped forward to offer Steren a friendly headbutt, but Aidan stepped between. "Steren's head is sore enough, I imagine," said Aidan.

Steren stood open-mouthed, still staring at Dobro. "I thought feechiefolk were made up," he said. "Just in stories."

Dobro was offended. "Made up? I'm as real as you are, brother!" He held out his hand as evidence. "Here, poke me. See, ain't I real?"

Steren reached out a finger and gingerly touched the back of Dobro's muddy hand.

It suddenly occurred to Dobro that he had said too much. Keeping civilizers ignorant of feechie ways—of feechies' very existence—was a cornerstone of the Feechie Code. "If it's all the same to you," said Dobro in a confidential tone, "let's keep this between us. Things work out better for us feechies when civilizers don't believe in us."

Steren nodded slowly, blankly. He wasn't likely to tell anyone about this meeting in any case. Nobody would believe him; everyone would probably think he was crazy.

"Truth is," Aidan explained, "Corenwald is crawling with feechiefolk."

Steren looked doubtful. "Then why haven't I ever seen one before now?"

"Because we're sneaky rascals," explained Dobro. "We stay in treetops and under the water when there's civilizers around."

"And they usually stay away from the civilized parts of the island anyway," added Aidan.

"We run things around the Feechiefen Swamp," said Dobro. "Then there's the hill feechies up north, the beach feechies on the east edge of the island. There's a pretty big band of feechiefolks lives in the Eechihoolee Marshes, down below the plain you call Bonifay. And the scouts go up and down the rivers all over the island, keeping an eye on things.

"If it makes you feel any better," Dobro said to Steren, who still looked skeptical, "there's plenty of feechiefolks don't believe civilizers is real either."

"So, Dobro, why aren't you at Feechiefen?" asked Aidan.

"Feechiefen's a nice place," said Dobro, "but I get itchy to see other things. I used to go to that meadow where you and me kilt that panther, but I given up on you."

Steren was growing more astonished by the minute. He had heard that Aidan killed a panther with a stone sling, but he had no idea a feechie had been involved.

"I don't live there anymore," said Aidan. "I live at the castle with King Darrow and Prince Steren here. I never knew how to get back in touch with you."

Dobro shrugged at this explanation. "Anyway, I was collecting eggs at the buzzard rookery, upriver from here. And I got so lonesome for my mama that I headed down the river right that minute. I was passing through this neighborhood when I heard a 'haaweee' over in the cane-brake. I moseyed over to join the fun, and a big old boar hog come crashing out of the cane. But it weren't a feechie hot after him. It was Aidan of the Tam. So I thought I'd say howdy."

"Which reminds me," said Aidan. "Your howdy cost me the biggest boar I've ever seen in these woods. We'll never catch him now."

"Aw, that hog ain't gone far," said Dobro.

Steren's astonishment was giving way again to peevish-ness, even jealousy at Aidan's friendship with this wild boy. "How do you know where the hog went?" he said.

"Boy," Dobro retorted, "I've forgotten more about swamp hogs than a civilizer will ever know. I know most of the hogs in this forest by first and last name."

Steren looked dubiously at the feechie, not sure whether to take that literally or not.

"If you was running that boar hog," Dobro continued, "I guarantee he's in the swamp cooling off. And I guarantee I know where." He pointed upstream. "There's a hog wallow not a quarter league up this way. He's laying under a gum tree in the greenbog just as sure as I'm standing here."

Dobro thought for a moment, and then his eyes took on an adventurous twinkle. "You know, I ain't been hog hunting in a good long while. What do you say we go catch that rascal?"

Aidan and Steren exchanged a look. "This hog wallow," said Aidan, "if it's in a swampy place, how can our horses get through?"

"They can't get through!" answered Dobro. "We'll leave them smelly things here. Besides," he added, "one old hog against three boys and two horses . . . That ain't a fair fight, is it?"

Steren shot a wry grin at Aidan and held out his spear. "If a fair fight's what we're after, we probably shouldn't take our spears either, eh, Aidan?"

Dobro shook his head and fixed a pitying look on the prince, as if he wondered how such a thick-headed person could possibly make it in the world. "Of *course* we're leaving your cold-shiny spears behind. It ain't right to go after critters that way. Critters can't make sharp things out of cold-shiny same as folks can."

"Did you get a look at that boar's white-shinies?" exclaimed Steren. He thrust his thumbs out from his jaws in imitation of the boar's razor-sharp tusks. "Do you expect he'll put them away to make sure it's a fair fight?"

Dobro reached over and tapped Steren's forehead with a gray-green finger. "Which would you rather have in a free fight? A pair of long tuskies or that brain of yours?" He gestured at the civilizers' spears. "I ain't gonna hunt the civilizer way."

"And without Dobro," Aidan said to Steren, "you and I don't have any chance of getting that hog."

Steren was still hesitant, but Dobro turned on his funny, swampy charm. "Come on, Sturn," he said. "Quit your mullygrubbing. Me and Aidan can't catch that hog without you."

"Come on, Steren," Aidan urged. "Who knows when we'll have another chance at a hog like that?"

Chapter Two

Greenbog

Dobro led the way up the River Trail, following the boar's tracks toward the hog wallow. He walked as silently as an owl in flight. But Dobro wasn't merely walking. He was hopping, or prancing, on his tiptoes—a quick, short step, followed by a long step; a quick, short step; a long step. Steren looked quizzically at Aidan, who merely shrugged. There was plenty he didn't know about the ways of feechiefolk.

Aidan and Steren considered themselves skilled trackers and experts at traveling stealthily through the forest. But the impossibly light fall of Dobro's bare feet—however strange his gait—made them seem lumbering flatfoots by comparison. Aidan looked down at the heavy boot prints he and Steren left in the sand. They seemed thick and clumsy, out of place among the sharp, crisp tracks left by the forest animals that passed that way— raccoon tracks like neat, tiny hands; delicate twin crescents of deer tracks; turkey tracks, sticklike and spindly. Even the massive boar left neat tracks in the sand—paired triangles a little broader than the deer tracks.

Looking down at the tracks, Aidan realized that Dobro wasn't leaving any. There were animal tracks and boot tracks, but there were no barefoot human tracks! Aidan caught up with Dobro and looked closely at his feet as he skipped along. He wasn't just walking on the tips of his long toes; he was walking on two toes per foot. With each step he dragged his toes, leaving a paired track that looked remarkably similar to a hog track.

"Dobro!" Aidan marveled. He was breaking the trackers' silence, but he couldn't help himself. "You're making hog tracks!"

Dobro quickly raised a finger to his lips but didn't stop hopping. "'Course I am," he whispered. "I ain't going to leave five-toe feechie prints where civilizers can see them. I got enough civilizers in my life already."

Aidan grabbed Steren's tunic. "Look," he whispered, pointing down at the trail, "half of those hog tracks are Dobro's." They watched Dobro take a few more steps. His irregular stride—short, long, short, long—was his way of mimicking a four-footed gait with only two feet. Suddenly the two civilizers were more interested in Dobro's unique skill than in the hunt itself. "Can you do any other tracks?" asked Steren.

"I can do wolf tracks," answered Dobro. On either foot he folded his small toe over the toe next to it and walked a few steps on the balls of his feet, producing the track of the red wolf—four toes over a single, broad foot-pad.

"Amazing," gasped Steren.

"I can do a bunny, too," said Dobro, "but it hurts a little bit." He cracked his knuckles, flipped upside down with his feet straight up in the air, and walked a few steps on his fingers. The palms of his hands didn't touch the ground; his whole weight was supported by two thumbs and two forefingers, his hands only a few inches apart. The flats of his thumbs made tracks like a rabbit's long thumper feet, and his forefinger tips made the tiny front paws.

The civilizers stood flabbergasted at Dobro's unheard-of talent. But the feechie was anxious to get on with the adventure. "That's enough trickifying," he announced. "Let's get on to the hog wallow."

They hadn't gone another fifty strides before the boar's tracks veered left and disappeared from the River Trail. "What'd I tell you?" whispered Dobro, pointing through the underbrush to a spot they couldn't see. "That boar hog is lazying in the greenbog."

Dobro double-checked the vine rope coiled at his waist, then scampered up the nearest loblolly bay. Aidan climbed the tree after him and motioned for Steren to follow. Steren was right behind, eager for adventure, but when Dobro leaped like a squirrel from the treetop to a nearby spruce pine, Steren stopped where he was. "He's crazy," he observed flatly.

Aidan chuckled. "You're right about that. But he still knows the best way to travel through a swamp. You just follow me. I'll follow him." Aidan edged out on the limb, leaped from the same spot Dobro had leaped from, and landed exactly where Dobro landed. Steren took a deep breath, closed one eye, and made the same soaring leap after him.

Flying from spruce pine to magnolia to laurel oak to bay tree, the civilizers grew more and more comfortable with the feechie's dizzying, exhilarating mode of crossing the bottomland. Here, forty feet or more above the forest floor, they were high above the mosquitoes and other biting, stinging bugs that would usually torment them in the swampy environs of the River Tam. And the air up so high was clearer and almost breezy compared to the heavy air at ground level.

When they paused a moment to rest, Aidan nudged Steren and pointed at the ground. "Look down," he whispered.

"I don't think so!" answered Steren. As exhilarating as this jaunt through the treetops had been, he wasn't completely over his fear of heights. "I'd better not look down."

But Aidan insisted, and when Steren looked, he saw that the dense, rough cover of hoorah bush and saw palmetto had given way to a rolling mat of vibrant yellowgreen. "A peat bog!" he exclaimed. Aidan and Dobro quickly shushed him, for if the boar had gone to its wallow as Dobro had said, he might be close enough to hear.

But Aidan couldn't begrudge Steren's enthusiasm. He hardly knew a more delightful place than a peat bog, where sphagnum moss piled layer on layer, blanketing the ground like a bright green blizzard. The mat was always growing, always layering on a new green surface, smothering the layers below, which partially rotted into a black, spongy muck. This bog had been growing for hundreds, perhaps thousands, of years, a fraction of an inch every year, and the green mat of moss the boys could see from the treetops floated a full three feet above the waterlogged soil that supported it.

While Aidan and Steren admired the rolling green sea below them, Dobro scouted the area for the hog. Swiftly and soundlessly, he soared from treetop to treetop.

It wasn't long before Dobro came swinging back to Aidan's and Steren's tree. "He's here, all right," he whispered. "Follow me." He led the way across the broad canopies of five gum trees before he gestured for them to be still. Aidan looked to the ground directly below him. There lay the hog on its side, as massive and black as the stump of one of the swell-buttressed gum trees that grew here in the bottomlands. The ground beneath his body was indented and rose around his mass on all sides, as if the hog were resting on a green feather mattress. Even from their perch in the tree, the hunters could hear the hog—a long, snuffling, grunting snore. His huge ear, flat and broad, flapped over his eye like a mule blinder. His legs lurched occasionally. In his dreams he was still running.

Dobro put one hand on Aidan's shoulder and the other on Steren's and pulled them in close. "Here's how it's going to work, boys: When I give you the sign, we all three going to drop on him. I'm gonna tie him up," whispered Dobro, "and your job's to hold him still." Steren shot a doubtful look in Aidan's direction.

"Aidan," continued Dobro, "you catch his left earflap. Sturn, you get the right'un."

Steren tried to butt in, but Dobro was making an important point and wouldn't be interrupted. "Once you grab aholt, you got to keep aholt." He clenched both fists in a gesture of determination. "Like you're squeezing all the goodie out of a duck tater." The civilizers had never squeezed a duck tater, but they got the idea nevertheless. "'Cause if you let go of your ear, things ain't gonna go too well for the feller's still got holt of the other ear.

"Aidan, you remember Chief Gergo, don't you?" Dobro held up three fingers in imitation of the three-fingered hand of his chieftain. "His hunting partner lost his holt on a boar hog about like this one." He chomped his teeth meaningfully and gave the civilizers a slow wink.

"Er, Dobro," said Prince Steren, trying to sound as nonchalant as possible, "couldn't we just rope him from here? I believe your rope will reach."

Dobro gave an exasperated sigh and shook his head. "Where's the sport in that?" he asked. And without waiting for an answer, he began counting for the jump signal: "One . . . two . . ."

Steren jumped up to protest Dobro's plan, but in doing so, he lost his footing and tumbled out of the tree. Dobro whistled as he watched the prince hurtle toward the moss twenty feet below. "That feller's so bloodthirsty he can't even wait for three!" he whooped. By the time Steren hit the turf, he had done a full flip. His feet landed hard on a soft spot in the ground, and he punched all the way through the green moss mat and into black muck up to his armpits.

The boar, of course, was awakened by the commotion and leaped to his feet with a piercing squeal and a roaring grunt. Or he tried to leap. The ground was so springy and yielding that he had to rock his great mass back and forth a couple of times to get his feet under him. Meanwhile, Aidan and Dobro flew out of the tree themselves to come to the rescue of the prince, who was struggling with little success to free himself from the deep peat while the boar decided whether to attack or flee.

Aidan landed just behind the hog's left shoulder; to his relief, he didn't go through the moss as Prince Steren had. Aidan grabbed hold of the hog's left ear and dug his boot heels into the soft turf. Dobro grabbed the hog's tail and held on like grim death. But, as Dobro had said earlier, it would take more than two hunters to bring down a hog that size. As the boar struggled to his feet, the ground beneath the struggling pile of hog and human rippled in waves, as if an earthquake had hit the bottomlands. The hog wheeled around, tossing his head in Aidan's direction, trying to slash his attacker to ribbons. Aidan managed to stay out of reach of the flashing tusks, but he wasn't sure how much longer he could keep his grip.

Dobro was having a hard go of it himself; he had already been kicked four or five times by the boar's flying hooves, and they were just getting started. But he wasn't ready to give up yet. "Squeeze that earflap!" called Dobro over the grunting and squealing. "Squeeze it like a duck tater."

"Steren!" called Aidan. "Steren, we need you!"

The hog was running across the bog now, crazed with terror and fury. Aidan had tried to dig in, but he was being dragged across the trembling turf. The skinny feechie was being trailed along behind the great boar like a flag behind a racing wagon, his feet hardly touching the ground.

Steren managed to free himself from the peat and charged across the greenbog to his friends' aid. He caught up just at the bog's edge. The hog had punched a foreleg through a soft spot in the turf and was struggling to free himself when Steren caught up and latched himself to the hog's right ear. The two big civilizers were able to pin the hog to the turf long enough for Dobro to whirl in and tie the hog's four legs together. The boar struggled against his bindings, squealing and harrumphing, thrashing his head back and forth, wanting to slash something—anything— wide open. But Dobro's knots were sure.

The feechie disappeared into a stand of hardwood near the edge of the greenbog and came back with an oak sapling he had hurriedly cut down with a stone saw he kept in his side pouch. "Tote-pole," he explained, and he began to stick the pole between the boar's knees just below the bindings, first the front knees, then through to the back. As he worked, he smiled at the civilizers. "Aidan, you got to tell Sturn about the time you come into the feechie camp on a tote-pole, just like this boar hog." Aidan laughed as he remembered the day he was captured by Rabbo Flatbottom and Jonko Backwater in the magnolia jumble near the Bayberry Swamp.

"Well, boys," said Dobro when the hog was secured to the tote-pole, "you look stout enough to get this big boy home without no help from a scrawny feechie like me. I'm ready to see my mama. Sturn, it was a pleasure. Aidan, don't be a stranger."

With that, the feechie boy disappeared into the forest. And the civilizers contemplated the long trip back to the horses with their massive, bristling, struggling prize.

Chapter Three

The Hunt Feast

ing Darrow's trophy room echoed with the chatter of a dozen separate conversations as the hunting party relived the previous day's adventure in Tamside Forest. Servants were still loading the tables with side dishes and making last-minute preparations before the arrival of the king and chief huntsmen and the presentation of the game.

A hunt feast was the least formal of the regular feasts held at Tambluff Castle. The feasters—noblemen and servants alike—didn't wear their usual festal robes, but rather their hunting tunics and muddy hunting boots. Hunting dogs milled about the room, eagerly awaiting their own portion of roast boar, for they had been participants in the hunt, too, and were entitled to a place at the feast.

Lord Cuthbert was the only feaster who had not been a member of the hunting party. The oldest of Corenwald's Four and Twenty Noblemen, Cuthbert had grown too blind to gallop through the forest. But he was still a regular at the hunt feasts. On this night he sat between Lord Cleland and Lord Radnor, who filled him in on the details of the hunt.

"Oh, I wish you could have been there, Bertie!" Cleland enthused. His eyes were alight with the excitement of the hunt. "There has never been such a boar hunt in Corenwald!"

"We were loping through the bottomlands," began Radnor, "the king and Wendell out in front, the boar dogs out in front of them." Old Cuthbert leaned forward in his chair and gazed into the middle distance as he pictured the scene he had witnessed so many times with his own eyes.

Radnor continued. "We hadn't been in the forest an hour before the dogs began to sing." Lord Cuthbert smiled wistfully at the memory of the dogs' throaty howl echoing in the cypress.

"We spurred our horses to catch up to the dogs," said Cleland, leaning forward in his chair as if he were still in the saddle.

"We found them in a little clearing," Radnor interrupted, unable to contain his enthusiasm, "and we saw that it wasn't one hog the dogs had jumped but a whole herd of them."

"A tribe of them," agreed Cleland. "A dozen or more

yearling pigs, seven or eight sows, and the biggest, blackest boar you ever saw."

"He looked more like a black bull than a boar, he was so big," added Radnor. "Except for those tusks. No bull ever had slashers like that."

Cleland picked up the story again. "So we were pressing this herd of hogs—hard after them—and it was one big tangle, I tell you. There were more hogs than dogs, and the hounds couldn't agree which one they should bay up."

Cuthbert listened intently. He imagined himself astride a hunting horse, crashing through the forests and swamps again.

"Meanwhile," said Radnor, "the big boar decided it was time to save his own bristly hide and let the women and children fend for themselves."

"Not very gentlemanly of him," remarked Cuthbert.

"Maybe not," answered Cleland, "but I've never been run down by a pack of boar dogs, so I won't say one way or another."

"He broke off from the herd and came barreling back through the dogs and horses and men," said Radnor, nearly out of his seat now. "Two of the dogs lunged at him, but he sent them flying. All the dogs stayed with the herd and let the daddy boar run back downriver."

Cuthbert's face fell with disappointment. The boar dogs' cowardice broke his heart.

"Meanwhile, Aidan and Prince Steren wheeled their horses around and lit out after the boar hog," continued Radnor.

Cuthbert snorted at the very idea. "Without dogs?" he huffed. "What did they think they were going to do with him if they caught him?"

"We're coming to that," answered Radnor. "We pressed the chase, and in the end King Darrow managed to kill a couple of the yearling pigs."

"Well, they'll be better eating than a tough old boar hog anyway," Cuthbert remarked by way of consolation.

"But that's not all," said Cleland. "When we got back to the castle, Aidan and Steren were waiting for us."

"And they had the big boar hog," added Radnor.

"Alive." Cleland paused for effect. "Somehow they had managed to catch the boar, tie him up, and carry him out of the woods on a sapling pole."

Cuthbert stared open-mouthed in Cleland's direction. "Impossible!" he said at last. "I don't believe you. Two boys can't catch a wild boar alive. Not without dogs."

"Hard to believe, Cuthbert, I know," said Radnor. "I wouldn't believe it either if I hadn't seen the hog with my own eyes."

"They won't say how they did it," added Cleland. "They say it's a secret."

Cuthbert slumped back in his chair, amazed by what he had been told.

"I tell you, that Errolson boy is something special," said Radnor. "Every time I turn around, he's done something I never thought anybody could do."

"Well, don't forget," said Cleland, "it wasn't just Aidan. The prince was with him too."

Radnor raised his eyebrows. "You tell me, Cleland. Do you really think the prince would have come back with the hog if he hadn't been with Aidan Errolson?"

The conversation was cut short by the sound of a hunting horn, the sign that King Darrow would be taking his place at the head table along with the chief huntsmen—the hunters who had most distinguished themselves in the previous day's outing. And to no one's surprise, the chief huntsmen for this feast were Prince Steren and Aidan Errolson.

As the king and the two boys entered the trophy room, the feasters cheered raucously and stomped their heavy boots. Even the hunting dogs howled and wagged themselves sideways. The courtiers had grown to love Aidan almost as much as they loved their king. In three short years, Aidan had made himself a regular at the head table during hunt feasts. Time after time, his fellow hunters had elected him chief huntsman and seated him at the king's right hand.

"There's a surprise!" called one of the noblemen. "Aidan Errolson is at the head table again!"

"It's the king of the forest!" shouted another. "And King Darrow too!"

The feasters were in a back-slapping good humor, ready to laugh and enjoy themselves, and they laughed heartily at these and similar jokes. King Darrow stretched his mouth into a smile—or something like it—but clearly he was not as amused as the other feasters at this line of jesting. In the past few months, Darrow had grown cold toward the young hero he had brought to his court. He no longer joined in when his noblemen sang Aidan's praises.

"One of these hunt feasts, we're going to put King Darrow at Aidan's right hand!" called another feaster.

Aidan watched Darrow's eyes narrow even as the lower half of his face continued to smile. He saw the king's jaw working as he ground his back teeth. Aidan quickly wiped the smile from his own face, hoping to discourage further jokes in this vein.

But immediately after the seating of the king and chief huntsmen came the presentation of the game, and with it came further reason for the king to be annoyed. Two liveried servants brought out the yearling pigs killed by Darrow's hunting party. Each was arranged in a bed of greenery on a silver platter, and each had an apple in its mouth. The feasters applauded politely as the pigs were placed on the head table in front of the king. They were nothing to be ashamed of, certainly. Two yearling pigs constituted a respectable bag for a morning's hunt.

But the applause swelled to a crescendo of cheering, whistling, and foot stomping when a trio of kitchen servants staggered into the trophy room under Steren's and Aidan's massive boar. It was roasted to a succulent brown, and in its snarling mouth an apple—the largest apple the cook could find—looked like a shriveled plum.

"Now that's a hog!" somebody shouted.

"Darrow should be ashamed of himself," joked Lord Grady, "killing those little piglets when a monster like that was prowling his forest!"

The head table, made of thick slabs of black walnut, sagged under the weight of the three hogs, not to mention the pots and platters of vegetables.

From where they sat, the noblemen could hardly see the king for the mountain of roast hog the servants had placed in front of him. "Say, what happened to King Darrow?" called Lord Cleland. "Are you still there, Your Majesty?"

Aidan stole a quick glance at Darrow. The king was looking down at his plate, his mouth set in a tight line. He wasn't even pretending to be amused now. Aidan stared down at the table, counting the tines on his forks, tracing the pattern on his dinner plate. It had been a hard few months for Aidan. The more he grew in the noblemen's favor, the harder it was to please his king.

"Look," laughed Lord Grady, "the great huntsman's ears are turning red!"

"Stop, Grady," came the voice of another nobleman. "You're embarrassing him." Aidan stared harder at his plate, praying that everyone's attention would soon shift elsewhere.

Suddenly, Aidan's plate lurched away from him like a boat that had drifted into a swift current. For a dizzying, disorienting moment, Aidan thought he was falling backward out of his chair. But Aidan wasn't tipping; the table was, tilting forward into the middle of the trophy room, crashing heavily onto its side. Earthenware dashed to pieces on the sandstone floor, and peas, carrots, and potatoes scattered in all directions. Candle stands clattered to the floor, and broken, extinguished candles lay among the debris. The hunting dogs boiled over the overturned table to get at the roasted hogs that lay broken on the floor.

Chapter Four

Aidan's Mission

Everyone stared in astonished silence at King Darrow, who stood in his place at the center of the head table. His face was still red from the exertion of flipping the thick walnut table and its heavy contents—no small feat for a man in his midsixties. His black eyes were flashing, and his hands were clenched into fists at his sides.

"I am Darrow," he said in a loud, clear voice that echoed around the trophy room. "I am king of Corenwald."

The courtiers, recovering a little, rose quickly to their feet out of respect for their king. Darrow put a booted foot on the edge of the overturned table and tipped it so it was completely upside down. The heavy clap of the tabletop on the floor scattered the dogs. The king stepped across the table and into the space between the two remaining tables. He stood in front of Lord Grady and spoke to him with clipped words. "I am your king."

Grady looked down at his hands, fumbling at his hunting tunic. "Yes, Your Majesty."

Darrow turned to the table behind him and walked to Lord Halbard. He reached across the table, grabbed a handful of Halbard's coat, and pulled him close until their noses almost touched. He searched Halbard's face, as if he no longer recognized his old friend. *"I . . . am . . . your . . . king!"* He spoke each word separately and distinctly, and his voice was raised to a near shout.

Halbard's eyes bulged with terror. "Y-yes, Your Majesty," he stuttered.

Meanwhile, the dogs had begun fighting over the carcass of Aidan's boar, and the growling, snapping, yelping mass tumbled into King Darrow and got tangled under his feet. The king let go of Halbard and kicked at the dogs. He caught two by the scruff of the neck, one with each hand, before they could scamper away. He lifted the two dogs up to his own eye level and, shaking with rage, screamed at them: *"I am your king!"* He dropped the dogs, and they slunk off whimpering, their tails between their legs.

Darrow now turned his attention to Aidan. He stalked toward the head table, unmindful of the potatoes and peas that stuck to the bottom of his boots with each step. Standing on the planks of the overturned table, he towered over Aidan. "I am Darrow of Tambluff!" he thundered.

"Yes, Your Majesty," Aidan answered, looking down at his boots. His father had taught him never to make eye contact with an aggressive bear; it seemed fitting advice at this moment.

Darrow leaned even closer, and Aidan could feel his hot breath on his forehead. "Look at me when I'm talking to you!" bellowed the king.

Aidan raised his eyes to look into his king's, and he was startled by what he saw. Darrow's eyes bulged out of their sockets. White showed all around the black pupils. Darrow saw the horror in Aidan's face. "How dare you look me in the eye?" he shouted, even though he was only inches away. "I am your king!"

Aidan wasn't sure where to look. He couldn't please the king by looking down; he couldn't please him by looking him in the eye. He fixed his eyes on Darrow's chin. "Yes, Sire. You are my king. I have never once forgotten."

King Darrow snorted. "You have forgotten many things, boy. You have forgotten every kindness I ever showed to you and your family. You have forgotten what you were when I brought you to Tambluff: a shepherd boy, the son of a father whose standing in the realm isn't what it used to be."

Darrow's low, contemptuous chuckle was interrupted by the clear voice of Prince Steren. "No, Father." Darrow wheeled around to face his son. But Steren wasn't cowed by his father's rage. "You are the one who has forgotten. Aidan's bravery saved your realm from the Pyrthen Empire. Is this your thanks for Aidan's service?"

"Quiet, you insolent pup!" spluttered Darrow. "You may be too foolish to see what this boy is doing, but I'm not." He shot a quick, scornful look at Aidan. "He wants to be king. From the day he got here, he's done everything he could to steal away the loyalty of my noblemen."

Aidan could feel hot resentment gather in a knot at his Adam's apple. But it wasn't only resentment he felt. He also felt the heartbreak and disappointment of injured love. No one in Corenwald was more devoted to King Darrow than Aidan was.

Darrow continued. "He has wheedled his way into your good graces, too, Steren, with his pretended friendship."

"Pretended?" yelped the prince. "How can you even say—"

Darrow raised his hand for silence. He was speaking more softly now. His rage seemed to have spent itself. "Quiet, Son. You must see. It's not my throne that's in danger. It's yours. I'll live out my days as high king of Corenwald." Darrow gestured toward Aidan behind him. "There's not much this schemer can do about that. But someday I will die. And do you think he'll just sit by and let you receive the crown of Corenwald without a fight?"

Darrow put a hand on either of Steren's shoulders. "You are a good and trusting soul. Too good. Too trusting."

The king turned and faced Aidan, who was too bewildered to speak. "I, too, have trusted too much." He spoke without emotion as he addressed Aidan. "I brought you into the bosom of my family. It would have been better to embrace a rattlesnake. At least a rattlesnake's venom works quickly. Yours is a slow poison."

Aidan had withstood Darrow's rage bravely. But this quiet insult was more than he could bear. He stood straight, his eyes fixed on Darrow's beard. But big tears welled in his eyes and rolled down his cheeks.

Darrow was unmoved. He spoke to Aidan with a steely evenness. "Save your tears, boy. A crocodile can cry too. But that doesn't mean it won't eat a man alive."

The king reached into a pouch that hung at his side and pulled out a piece of folded palmetto paper with a broken wax seal. Without prelude or explanation he began to read it:

Your Majesty—

I write to warn you: Your most dangerous enemy dwells under your roof. Beware the youngest son of Errol.

He has convinced himself that he is the Wilderking of ancient prophecy—the rightful occupant of your throne. His every action is calculated to convince your courtiers of the same. His claim to have killed a panther with a stone is a claim on the throne of Corenwald—a blatant reference to the Wilderking Chant:

> *With a stone he shall quell the panther fell,*
> *Watch for the Wilderking!*

He claims friendship with feechiefolk as part of a scheme to build a legend in keeping with the Wilderking prophecy.

At the mention of feechiefolk, Steren gasped, remembering his own run-in with Dobro Turtlebane the day before. But Darrow paid him no attention and kept reading the last paragraph of the letter.

Your Majesty, it pains me to accuse a fellow Corenwalder of treason. But it pains me more to think that my king would be nurturing a traitor under his own roof.

Yours sincerely,
A loyal subject

All the color drained from Aidan's face as the king read. It was a lie, of course, but it contained just enough truth to make it hard to answer. Yes, he had come to believe that he was destined to be the Wilderking, but that realization had been thrust upon him. He had never wanted such a destiny, had certainly never schemed to put himself in that position. Yes, he claimed to have killed a panther; yes, he claimed to know feechiefolk. But never had he shown (or even felt) anything less than perfect loyalty to the House of Darrow. He stood mute under the glare of his king.

Darrow turned to the assembled courtiers. "See?" he said, gesturing at Aidan with one hand and waving the letter in the other. "He doesn't even deny it."

For the first time since Darrow's outburst, one of the noblemen spoke. "Your Majesty," said Lord Aethelbert cautiously, "these are very serious accusations. An anonymous letter is not the same thing as evidence."

Darrow fixed Aethelbert with a withering glare. "Ah yes, Aethelbert. On the boy's side, are you?" He looked around the trophy room at the other noblemen. "Does anyone else wish to throw in his lot with these two traitors?"

The room remained silent. No one else was willing to take on the king when he was in this irrational frame of mind. Aidan looked imploringly from face to face, but no one, not even Steren, would meet his gaze.

Finally Aidan spoke. His voice was choked with emotion. "I have only ever loved you, my king." Darrow gazed blankly at him. Aidan tried again. "Your Majesty, I have desired only to serve you and your house." Darrow looked away, staring into the distance as if he had heard nothing.

"Command me, my king." Aidan's tone was plaintive. "How can I prove my loyalty to you?"

King Darrow still stared into the distance, but his eyes narrowed slightly as he mulled his options. Aethelbert was right. He didn't have hard evidence against the boy, even if he was sure of his guilt. Still, evidence or no evidence, he couldn't afford to have the boy at his court any longer. He believed what he had said to Steren: Even if the boy weren't a threat to Darrow's own kingship, he was a serious threat to his hopes for Steren. And yet he couldn't have the boy killed or banished. The Four and Twenty Nobles would never let him get away with that. Maybe he could use the boy's professed loyalty against him.

At last the king turned to Aidan. "I suppose you've noticed I suffer bouts of melancholy."

Aidan just listened, choosing not to acknowledge how obvious the king's depressive episodes had become.

"My medics and chemists have tried everything that might offer me some relief," continued the king. "But nothing seems to help. There is one last treatment—a certain cure—but they lack the only ingredient."

"Is it something I can get for you?" asked Aidan hopefully.

"Perhaps you can. The old lore promises one sure cure for melancholy: the essence of the frog orchid. Bring me a live frog orchid, and I will have no reason to doubt your loyalty."

"A frog orchid?" barked Lord Cleland. "I know a little of the old lore, too, Darrow. The frog orchid grows only in the depths of the Feechiefen Swamp." Darrow nodded knowingly but without apparent concern. Cleland continued. "Nobody has ever come back alive from the Feechiefen Swamp!"

But Aidan was relieved to have been offered the chance to prove his loyalty, even if the offer came in the form of a seemingly impossible task. "I'll leave first thing in the morning."

Lord Cleland wouldn't let it lie. "You're sending Aidan to his death, and you know it!" he protested.

"You weren't so squeamish three years ago, when the boy offered to fight the giant on the Bonifay Plain," Darrow retorted. "What was it you said, Cleland? 'If the boy wants to die for his country, why not let him?'"

Cleland was ashamed of the words he spoke the first time he ever met Aidan Errolson on the battlefield at Bonifay. But he couldn't deny them.

"Well, if the boy wants to die for his king," continued Darrow, "why not let him?"

But Aidan wasn't there to hear this exchange. He was already headed toward his sleeping quarters to pack a bag for his trip to Feechiefen.

Aidan was nearly finished packing when the door swung open and Prince Steren stepped into the room. He looked at the backpack on Aidan's bed, and his face filled with horror. "You're not really . . ." he began. "Into the Feechiefen?"

Aidan didn't answer but kept packing.

"Don't do this," Steren pleaded. "You know how Father is. Tomorrow he will have forgotten all about this. Why don't you go away for a few days? Go see your father and brothers at Longleaf. Father will be all right."

"It's been a long time since your father's been all right," Aidan answered. "Toward me anyway. He's lost faith in me, Steren. I can't stay here if my king has no faith in me. Yet I cannot bear to leave the court of Darrow. I must complete this quest."

Then, almost as an afterthought, Aidan added, "Besides, if the essence of the frog orchid really does cure your father's melancholy, that will be a service to the whole kingdom."

"But nobody ever comes back from the Feechiefen," Steren persisted. "What makes you think you will?"

Aidan rolled back his sleeve to expose a red scar in the shape of an alligator on his right forearm. "That's the feechiemark," he said. "It means any feechie I meet is obliged by their code of honor to be a friend to me."

"Like Dobro," Steren observed.

"That's right," answered Aidan. "By the providence of the One God, I believe the feechies will see me through the Feechiefen."

"Do you even know how to get into the Feechiefen?" Steren asked.

"Just what we all learned in geography lessons," said Aidan. "Follow the Tam to Last Camp and turn south. You can't miss it. But I'll stop by Longleaf tomorrow to see what my brother Jasper can tell me. He knows the old lore backward and forward."

Both boys were silent for a moment, then Steren spoke up with the determined voice of a person not accustomed to being told no. "I'm coming with you, Aidan."

Aidan shook his head. "No, Steren. This is my mission."

"But you're my best friend," Steren insisted. "I can't let you face that kind of danger alone."

"We may be best friends," said Aidan, "but your responsibilities to Corenwald outweigh your friendship to me. You're the crown prince, King Darrow's only heir. You can't go galloping off to the Feechiefen Swamp."

Steren saw Aidan's point. "I'll pray for you, Aidan," he said. "Every day." He turned to leave, then stopped.

"Was any of it true, Aidan? About you believing that you're the Wilderking?"

It was a hard question for Aidan to answer. So he answered another question instead: "No one has ever been more loyal to the House of Darrow than I am."

Chapter Five

Home Again

Aidan was about to turn his horse off River Road and into the cart path leading to the manor house when his brother Percy burst through the gate at a dead run and lurched to a stop in front of him. Percy was eighteen now, and his responsibilities at Longleaf Manor were growing as he moved into manhood. But in his enthusiasms, he was as boyish as ever.

"Aidan!" he shouted breathlessly, not even bothering to say hello to the brother he hadn't seen in nearly a year. "You've got to see this!" He grabbed the horse by the bridle and, horse and brother in tow, ran down the trail that led to the River Tam.

Aidan was anxious to see his father, his other brothers, and the old home place after so long an absence. But it was hard not to be carried away by Percy's enthusiasm. "What's at the river?" he asked. But as soon as the question was out of his mouth, the river came into view and he could see for himself.

Around the upstream bend a huge timber raft slid along the surface of the water. It must have been constructed from forty full-grown pine trees lashed together, and they made a floating floor more than half the size of the floor in King Darrow's great hall. At the front of the raft, two men wearing buckskin and coonhide caps were straining at a long pole that reached into the water. The pole was an oar-sweep—a forty-foot-long paddle whittled from a single pine sapling and balanced on a waist-high oar bench. In the spring of the year, when the water was high, a skilled rafthand could stand at the back of a raft and, using that one long oar, guide a hundred tons of pine trees around any bend or whirl the River Tam might offer.

But these obviously weren't skilled rafthands. The back of the raft was where the front was supposed to be, and the front was where the back was supposed to be. They were drifting down the river in a slow spin, in spite of their efforts with the oar-sweep. They were utterly at the mercy of the current. Aidan shielded his eyes against the high sun and peered upriver at the vast bulk of pine logs lumbering toward them, sideways now. "Who are those people?" he asked.

"A couple of gator hunters up from Last Camp," answered Percy. "They bought a load of logs from a farmer clearing a field above Hustingreen." The Errolsons watched one of the gator hunters get knocked into the river by the swinging oar-sweep, and Percy couldn't help chuckling while the other hunter, the bearded one, fished him out. "They thought it would be a good idea to build the logs into a raft and float them down to Big Bend."

"Big Bend?" snorted Aidan. "I'll be amazed if they make it around the next bend. How do they expect to make it all the way to Last Camp?"

The Errolsons watched the approaching vessel get closer. For the moment it was oriented correctly: bow in the front, stern in the back. But it was already going into another rotation. "Ebbe was at Hustingreen this morning when they came barreling through," said Percy, smiling at the old house servant's description of the scene. "Said they had the whole village in an uproar. They came shooting out of the upper shoals like a hog on ice, taking out everything in their way. Smashed up a few fishing skiffs, barely missed the ferryboat, and the whole time those two swampers are shouting and yelling at one another, riding that sweep like a bucking horse." Percy pointed at the raft and chuckled. "About like they're doing now."

The raft was less than a hundred strides away, and they could hear the hunter-raftsmen yelling at one another.

"Pull to the starboard!" called the one with a beard.

"I *am* pulling to the starboard!" shouted the other, obviously irritated.

"Nah, starboard's the other way when the boat's going backerds."

The men's faces were red from yelling and pulling. The fact that they pulled in opposite directions didn't help.

"Who made you cap'n anyway?"

"Somebody's got to be cap'n, and I reckon it ought to be the one with some sense."

The raftsmen had stopped pulling in opposite directions. Now they were pushing one another. The raft, meanwhile, was booming down on Longleaf landing.

Percy cupped his hands around his mouth and shouted to be heard over the men's bickering. "Ahoy there, sailor men!"

The raftsmen, who had stopped paying attention to where they were going, were surprised to hear a human voice on this lonely stretch of river—and especially so close. They were stern-first again, and from their post at the oar bench, they were only a few feet away from the Errolsons.

"Throw me a line," offered Percy, "and I'll tie you up." The bearded raftsman, the self-appointed captain of the vessel, let go of the oar-sweep and bent to sling the heavy rope that coiled at the near corner of the raft. At the same time, the sweep grounded itself in the deep river mud and levered the other rafter off his feet. The force of the massive raft against the long oar-sweep catapulted the hapless gator hunter well up the bank and then snapped the pole like a dry twig.

The captain sighed as he watched Aidan help his partner to his feet. "Well, Floyd, I reckon that's one way to disembark from a timber raft." He hopped onto the bank while Percy secured the raft with a hitch knot around a cypress tree. "But it's a sight too show-offy for me." He shook Percy's hand, then Aidan's. "I'm

Massey," he said, "cap'n of this ship. And the gymnast here is Floyd."

Floyd shook hands with the Errolsons too. "Massey ain't no more cap'n than a muskrat is," he said, smiling, "but he's right about one thing. My name's Floyd."

"We're the Errolsons," said Aidan. "He's Percy, and I'm Aidan."

"Errolsons?" exclaimed Massey. He seemed a little disappointed. "Does that mean we ain't no further down-river than Longleaf?"

"Afraid so," answered Percy.

"Ha!" barked Floyd. "I told you, Massey!" He looked at Aidan and Percy. "The cap'n here was sure we was just around the corner from Big Bend."

Massey grumbled something about the difference between a captain and a navigator, directing a significant look at Floyd. But he thought it best to change the subject as quickly as possible. "Wait a minute," he said. "You said your name was Aidan?"

"Yessir," answered Aidan.

"Aidan Errolson?"

"Hey," interrupted Floyd. "You're the feller killed the Pyrthen giant."

"Well," began Aidan, "he wasn't really a giant . . ."

"We was there," said Floyd excitedly, "both of us."

"And if that weren't a giant," said Massey, "I ain't never seen a giant." He swelled his chest up, rose up on his tiptoes, and stalked around a few steps. Floyd twirled his coonskin cap above his head, pantomiming Aidan's motion with a sling, and then let an imaginary stone fly at

Massey. Massey staggered in a circle and then flopped down in the sand in imitation of the epic fall of Greidawl, the Pyrthen champion.

"You've growed since then," remarked Floyd.

Percy reached a hand down to help Massey to his feet. "Get up, Greidawl," he said. "And you two come eat dinner with us."

"Supper too," added Aidan. "You can't go anywhere until you get a new oar-sweep. We'll get Carver to start working on one right away. You can leave in the morning."

"Why, sure," said Massey. "We'd be proud to stay the night at the House of Errol." And with that, the foursome headed up the path to the manor house.

Chapter Six

Home-Cooked Meal

When the Errolsons arrived at the manor house with Massey and Floyd, Ebbe eyed the two alligator hunters suspiciously. From their buckskin garb he recognized them as the raftsmen who had wreaked havoc on the Hustingreen riverfront earlier in the day. Ebbe had always been more concerned with the dignity of the House of Errol than Errol or his sons had ever been. He felt much put-upon when one of the Errolsons—usually Percy—dragged in characters like these two river rats for him to wait on.

But Percy, pretending not to notice Ebbe's annoyance, smiled broadly at the head servant. "Ebbe," he said, "these old boys could use a wash-up before dinner, and they might like to rest their bones a few minutes before we eat." He nudged Floyd. "Rafthanding is hard work."

"So I have observed," Ebbe answered icily, looking at Floyd's breeches, still wet from his dip in the river. The hunters, unaccustomed to such withering propriety, held their coonskin caps in their hands and studied the floor. The pale, skinny house servant struck terror in the hearts of these men who made their livelihood wrestling alligators with their bare hands.

"So maybe you could show them to a couple of the spare bedrooms and dip them up some washbowls," suggested Percy.

Ebbe waited a long second, blinked slowly, and with a formal smile answered, "Certainly."

Ebbe had begun to turn on his heel when Percy added, "And you might want to say hello to Aidan too."

Ebbe bobbed stiffly in Aidan's direction. "Master Aidan."

Aidan smiled at the stuffy old servant. "Hello, Ebbe."

Ebbe didn't trust Aidan much more than he trusted the alligator hunters. He had been attached to the House of Errol since before the boy was born, had seen the boy in diapers, seen him cry when he fell down, seen him waste away whole days in boyish daydreams. He had heard the other servants' whispered talk of Aidan being the Wilderking, and he didn't think it was proper at all— not at all. The whole thing started the day Aidan claimed to have killed a panther in the bottom pasture. But Ebbe had gone to the bottom pasture himself, had taken the boy's place watching the sheep—which, as Ebbe often pointed out, wasn't part of his job in the first place—and he saw for himself that there was no dead panther in the bottom pasture.

But still the servants talked, about the boy killing a giant and routing the Pyrthen army almost single-handedly, about other accomplishments they took to be signs the boy was indeed the Wilderking. But what did the other servants know, thought Ebbe, as he led the alligator hunters down the hall without speaking a word to them. The other servants would believe anything. They even believed in feechiefolk.

Percy left for the woodshop to get Carver started on a new oar-sweep for Massey and Floyd. Aidan knocked on the door of his father's library. "Father?" he called. Pushing the door open, he was surprised to see his father struggling to his feet, both hands on a walking stick. Errol gave his son a weary smile, and as he walked toward the door, Aidan noticed his father's limp had worsened. He looked more haggard and world-weary than he had six months earlier, when Aidan last saw him; it was the last time Errol had visited Tambluff Castle. Errol's trips to the court of King Darrow had grown less frequent as his health declined. Or perhaps, as Aidan suspected, his father's health had declined because his visits to the court had grown less frequent.

"You've grown," Errol observed as he embraced his son. "King Darrow must be feeding you well."

"He feeds me very well," answered Aidan, "but still I miss Moira's cooking."

Errol laughed and put his arm around Aidan's shoulder, as much for support as out of affection for his son. "Moira will be glad to hear her kitchen compares so favorably to the king's."

Aidan looked down at his father's walking stick. "How are you feeling, Father?"

Errol sighed. "These old battle wounds are troubling me. The rheumatism has crept into my bad leg." Leaning on Aidan, he hobbled to the nearest chair and sat down heavily. Aidan could feel his own eyes grow wet with the sadness of seeing his father, always so hale and strong, carrying himself now like an old man.

"I had hoped you'd come to Darrow's hunt two days ago," said Aidan. Then, thinking of his father's ailing state, he quickly added, "Or at least to the hunt feast."

"So I gathered from your letters," answered Errol. "So I gathered. But I never got an invitation from the king." He looked vacantly out the window. "There was a time when I was free to come and go as I pleased at Tambluff Castle," he said quietly. "But no more."

Aidan remembered King Darrow's remark the night before, when he referred to Errol as a man "whose standing in the realm isn't what it used to be."

Errol patted his left leg, his bad leg. "I've had this limp for thirteen years now, since the Pyrthens' fourth siege of Tambluff," he remarked. "It's never bothered me much. It always seemed a small price to pay for freedom, a small enough tribute to a king I loved, a king who loved his kingdom like a father loves his family." He stared into the distance. "But now this old battle wound is a misery to me."

Aidan and Errol sat in silence for a few awkward seconds before Aidan changed the subject. "Brennus wrote. Said Gemma was having a baby."

"That's right," answered Errol, brightening at the prospect. "They've been married over a year now. It's time they gave me a grandchild."

"He said in his letter that he cleared another field for indigo," added Aidan.

"That farm of his will be another Longleaf before you know it," said Errol. Though he had hoped that his eldest would stay and raise his family on Longleaf Manor, he was proud of the young man's initiative. "You know how your brother works." He paused a moment, then chuckled. "Your brother Brennus anyway. Your brother Percy is another matter altogether. It's not that he minds working; it's just that he likes so many other things better, it's hard to get a whole day's work out of him. This is the son who decides to stay on the farm." He shook his head and smiled. "But he's good company. And I'm going to need it when Jasper starts at the university in the fall."

"I'd almost forgotten," said Aidan. "We'll be together again." Tambluff University was just around the corner from the castle drawbridge.

"But I don't know what the professors at the university are going to be able to teach that boy," Errol remarked. "He knows the old lore better than anybody I've ever seen—except the Truthspeaker, maybe. He's read every book in the library."

Father and son both fell silent. Both were thinking of the other Errolson, the missing one. Maynard had disappeared two years earlier, less than a year after Aidan moved to Tambluff. He went out hunting in the Eastern Wilderness and never came back.

Everyone had given Maynard up for dead. That was just the way of the Eastern Wilderness: sometimes people went out and never came back. It was a vast and perilous place. Only Errol still held out hope for his son's safe return. But it was a hope fueled by a father's love and blind faith—not by any reasonable expectation that

Maynard could possibly be alive. But even Errol's faith had begun to waver. Every day he looked a little grayer.

Aidan had already decided not to tell his father the whole story of why he was headed downriver. He would find out soon enough, whether Aidan told him or not. Now that he saw his father's troubled state, Aidan was even more convinced it would do more harm than good to explain that King Darrow had sent him on a fool's errand, an impossible mission he didn't expect Aidan to survive. "King Darrow has sent me on a mission down the river."

"Hmmm . . ." said Errol. "Sounds important." There was a pause. Aidan looked down at his boots. Errol pressed him. "Too important for you to tell your father about?"

Aidan was between a rock and a hard spot. It would be a disaster to tell his father that he was headed alone into the very heart of the Feechiefen Swamp. Father would be worried sick, and rightly so. He would probably try to stop him from going, command him as his father to stop this insane quest. And Aidan wouldn't do that. To quit his quest would mean self-banishment. King Darrow had ordered him not to return without the frog orchid.

Not to tell, however, would be a slap in Father's face. Until recently, Errol had been one of Darrow's chief advisers. The king did almost nothing without Errol's knowledge. Had Darrow now entrusted Aidan with a task that was too secret for Errol to know about? Had Errol's fifteen-year-old son surpassed him in the king's confidence?

Errol saw the struggle on Aidan's face. "I understand," he said. "I won't ask you to betray your king's trust." Aidan nodded his head. But he couldn't meet his father's gaze. The silence between father and son was mercifully broken by the clanging of Moira's dinner bell.

‡ ‡ ‡

Moira was bringing around pies she had made from plum preserves, but as usual, Percy was so busy talking to the guests that he had hardly touched his dinner of venison and sweet potatoes.

"So if you needed timber at Last Camp," Percy asked Massey, "why didn't you just cut down some of the trees down there? Hustingreen to the Big Bend is a long float."

Massey straightened in his chair and answered self-importantly, "I ain't a timber cutter," as if felling trees were beneath the dignity of an alligator hunter.

"Well, if you don't mind my saying so," observed Percy, "you aren't much of a rafthand either." Percy's twin Jasper, who had taken off from his studies to eat dinner, couldn't help but snicker. Ebbe, standing behind Lord Errol's chair, raised the back of his hand to his mouth as if to conceal a laugh.

Lord Errol intervened, mindful of his guests' feelings. "Why do you need a raft of timber at Last Camp?"

"We're building a stockade," answered Floyd.

"A stockade?" asked Errol. "Who would attack hunters and trappers?"

"We don't know," said Floyd. He was grimly serious now. "That's what's got us worried."

"Somebody wants us gone from Last Camp," explained Massey. "They hide in the woods and shoot up the camp with arrows, throw spears in amongst us."

"Just the other day," said Floyd, "Massey was leaning up against a tree resting after a day-long hunt, when a spear come sailing in and stuck in the tree just above his head."

"Parted my ever-loving hair like a Tambluff dandy," added Massey. With his right hand he showed the motion of the spearpoint, imitating the noise of an arrow in flight striking a tree: "*Sssssssssst-thwonnnngg!*"

"I never seen such a near miss," said Floyd.

"Was it a near miss," asked Jasper, "or a warning shot? A man who can part your hair with a spear can kill you just as easily."

"Well, whatever it was," said Massey, "near miss, warning shot, or friendly hello, we're building ourselves a fort."

"And we're building it strong," added Floyd.

The diners returned to their plum pies. Errol, poking at his rather than eating it, finally asked the question he always asked anyone from the Eastern Wilderness. "Have you seen my son Maynard?"

Massey and Floyd looked at each other, then at Errol. "No sir," answered Floyd. "Why?" Errol didn't answer, only picked more at his pie.

Mostly to fill the dead air, Percy asked, "Do you boys ever run into plume hunters in the Eastern Wilderness?"

Massey looked a little shocked, as if someone had asked him if any of his friends were grave robbers, but Massey did his best to answer politely. "No, plume hunters know they ain't welcome at Last Camp, and they stay clear of us in the forest too."

Errol's face went from red to purple, and he pounded the table. "Percy!" he shouted. "How can you sit at my table and even speak of plume hunters?" He pushed his pie away. His appetite was ruined. "The vile criminals— how I'd like to get my hands on a few plume hunters!

"It's a mean business, plume hunting. Trading a heron or an egret's life for two feathers on a dandy's hat—to pluck a dead bird's plumes and leave the rest of it on the ground to rot. Nobody gets fed. Nobody gets clothed. Just feathers for a dandy's hat."

It was a good thing, thought Aidan, that his father hadn't been to Tambluff lately. His old-fashioned frontier sensibilities would have been shocked by the extravagance of the latest spring fashions. The Pyrthen Empire may have been Corenwald's bitterest enemy, but the Pyrthens still defined clothing styles for the known world, and wealthy Corenwalders worked hard to mimic the Pyrthens' outlandish dress. Men and women alike, bowing and nodding their elaborately plumed hats at one another, bobbed up and down Tambluff's High Street like tall ships under sail.

"That's not the worst of it either," continued Errol. "The navy stopped a smugglers' ship near Middenmarsh last week. They found bales and bales of plumes." He paused a minute, finding it hard to finish saying what everyone at the table could figure out for himself. "Those plumes were headed for Pyrth. There's hardly a plume bird left on the continent. The Pyrthens have used them all up for hats and horse bridles. So somebody is sending them ours . . . for as long as they last."

Errol wiped his mouth with his napkin and stood to leave. It was clear from his abrupt manner that he was finished talking about plume hunting. "Percy," he said, "go get a field wagon and carry me around to see how the melons are coming along."

Chapter Seven

The Old Lore

idan spent the rest of the afternoon in the library with Jasper. He was hungry for any old lore related to the frog orchid, the Feechiefen Swamp, or the ways of the feechiefolk.

The two brothers leaned over a huge map of Corenwald, stretched out to cover the whole library table. Here was the kingdom in its entirety. In the north, the high mountains towered over dales, hollows, and high country lakes. A different kind of wildness prevailed there—not the swampy, sandy wildness of Aidan's native haunts, but a wildness of crags and rocks and waterfalls, of elk and brown bears three times the size of a man.

South of the mountain range rose the foothills, where miners scratched out a living under the ground. A low plateau stretched across the middle of the island. This was

Corenwald's breadbasket. Its lush and rolling land was sectioned into farms arranged in tidy grids. Here the map was dotted thickly with villages and towns. Here the world seemed orderly and safe.

At the bottom edge of the plateau, the capital city of Tambluff, the gleaming jewel of Corenwald, was tucked into a bend of the River Tam. From there, to the south, east, and west, the land dropped to a low and sandy plain where the rivers meandered slowly, taking their sweet time on the last long leg of their journey to the sea.

On the western coast, the chief city was the deep-harbored port of Middenmarsh. The first settlers of Corenwald landed there and radiated east across the Bonifay Plain and toward the River Tam. In the southwest quarter of the island, the land drained by the Eechihoolee River, the population was sparser than in the center of the island. But still, the map showed farms and villages stretching as far down as the southern coast, where oranges and lemons grew.

The swampy heart of Corenwald was in the south and east, where the River Tam flowed. Here the map grew murky indeed. Flowing south from Tambluff, the river rolled through Hustingreen, then along the edge of Longleaf Manor. But as the river flowed through the Eastern Wilderness, the map showed nothing else for leagues and leagues. No village, no settlement, no farmstead. Beyond Longleaf, there was only one more marking on the map. The river made a looping bend before turning east for its last push to the sea. This was Big Bend. And situated on the very bottom of the bend, on the north side of the river, was Last Camp. It was the last out-post of civilization in the Eastern Wilderness.

To the south of Last Camp, across the river, the bottom right corner of the map was simply labeled "Feechiefen Swamp." There was no further detail—no islands, no waterways, not even an outline of the swamp. No one really knew what lay beyond Last Camp. Jasper dug up every map he could find. Pretending to look for something in the Eastern Wilderness, Aidan let his eyes wander down to the southeastern extremity of each map. But each was the same. No matter how detailed the map, the Feechiefen was a big blank. As far as the mapmakers were concerned, Feechiefen was beyond the edge of the world. The only thing to be learned from the maps was what Aidan already knew: To get to Feechiefen, he would have to go to Last Camp and turn south. And pray to the One God.

Jasper rolled up the last of the maps. Aidan remarked, "Lord Cleland mentioned something called the frog orchid. Do you know anything about a frog orchid?"

"Ah, the frog orchid," answered Jasper. "Not one of the more well-known bits of lore." He dug into the scrolls again and pulled out a manuscript. Jasper was loving this; someone was interested in the old lore he loved so much, someone he could instruct and show off for. He unrolled the manuscript and ran his finger down the elaborately scripted lines. "Here it is," he said eagerly, and he began reading aloud:

In deepest swamp, the house of bears,
An orchid in the spring appears

On oaken limb around a pond
As black as night and round as sun.
It floats in air, a ghostly white.
It soars and leaps like frog in flight.
And in the orchid's essence pure
Is melancholy's surest cure.

Aidan whistled. "What on earth does that mean?"

Jasper shrugged. "A lot of the lore-masters think it doesn't mean anything," he said. "They think it's just a little song. After all, if nobody's ever come back alive from Feechiefen Swamp, who could have written it?"

"But let's say it does mean something," said Aidan, undeterred. His king had sent him in search of the frog orchid, and he was going to make the attempt, whatever the lore-masters might think about it. "Let's say it actually does give clues for finding the frog orchid. What could it mean?"

Jasper's brow creased with concentration. "'In deepest swamp, the house of bears.' What would be a house of bears?"

Aidan thought. "A cave? A bee tree? A canebrake?" He shook his head. "I don't know. Could be a lot of things." He turned to the next line of the chant: "'An orchid in the spring appears.' That makes sense, at least."

Jasper picked up the chant. "'On oaken limb around a pond / As black as night and round as sun.'"

"So the orchid is black? And round?" asked Aidan.

"No," Jasper answered. "I think that's the pond where it grows. The pond is round and black." Jasper returned to the next two lines: "'It floats in air, a ghostly white. / It soars and leaps like frog in flight.'"

Aidan's head was swimming. "So it floats? I thought it grew on oak trees. And since when did frogs fly?" He was getting discouraged. No wonder the lore-masters thought the Frog Orchid Chant didn't mean anything.

Jasper shrugged again. "That's the way it is with the old lore. Sometimes you run across something that seems like it couldn't possibly make sense." Then he added, "But then one day you find out it was true and right all along."

"What other feechie lore do you have in here?" Aidan asked, thumbing at some of the manuscripts on a reading stand.

Jasper walked to the shelf where he kept scrolls of children's stories and folk tales. "Let's see," he muttered. "I had a scroll here that Maynard used to come in and read quite often."

"Maynard?" said Aidan, surprised. "When did Maynard ever come to the library?"

"Oh, he and I spent many evenings in here reading together after you went to Tambluff," said Jasper.

Aidan was floored. "I just never knew Maynard to be interested in the old lore or in anything the rest of us were interested in. What sort of thing did he read?"

"Feechie tales mostly." Jasper gave up looking for the scroll of feechie lore, which obviously wasn't in its place. He noticed the look of open-mouthed wonder on Aidan's face. "I know, I know. Maynard always thought you were lying about the feechie in the bottom pasture.

He acted like feechie talk was the craziest thing he had ever heard of. But people can change.

"After you went to Tambluff," Jasper continued, "Maynard tried harder to be a good son and a good brother. He even took your place watching sheep in the bottom pasture for awhile. It was like he was trying to make something up to you, or to Father."

Jasper shook his head. "I think that's part of the reason Father has taken Maynard's death so hard."

Aidan looked out the window. Father was returning from the melon field with Percy. He looked very old. "Poor Father," Aidan whispered.

Chapter Eight

River Run

The morning sky was still pink with the sun's first rays when the alligator hunters boarded their raft. A night's rest in real beds had rejuvenated them, and they were eager to take on the river again. The previous day's difficulties seemed a distant dream.

Besides, they now had an extra rafthand. They had convinced Aidan to float with them to the Big Bend. They would need him, for they had another oar-sweep now. Carver, besides replacing the broken oar-sweep, had carved them a second one and built another oar bench in the front of the raft. It would make the raft more maneuverable, but it also meant they could use an extra pair of hands. For his part, Aidan couldn't resist the adventure of a raft trip down the river, even if he could get to Last Camp more quickly on the Overland Trail. Besides, he liked the alligator hunters, and he preferred not to travel alone if he didn't have to.

Errol rode down to the landing with Percy and Jasper to see his youngest son off. He didn't say much. The only smile he could muster looked tired and sad. Somehow he sensed that Aidan's journey was to be much more perilous than he had let on. When everything was in order, just before Aidan stepped onto the raft, Errol caught him by the tunic and enfolded him in his arms. The strength of his father's embrace nearly squeezed the breath out of Aidan. There was plenty of life left in the old man, despite his haggard, world-weary appearance. That knowledge heartened Aidan and strengthened him for his journey.

"God go with you, Aidan," said Errol. "And be careful." Then, where no one else could hear, he whispered, "I couldn't bear to lose another son."

Aidan embraced his brothers and exchanged farewells. Jasper handed him a small cage containing one of his homing pigeons. "Take this with you," he said, "and send us a note when you get where you're going." Aidan knew he wouldn't be taking a pigeon into the Feechiefen, but he took the bird with the intention of sending his family a note from Last Camp.

Aidan joined Massey and Floyd on the raft. Jasper and Percy untied the heavy mooring ropes from the cypress trees and tossed them onto the raft timbers. The alligator hunters leaned against the sweeps, pushing off from the landing, and Aidan felt the Tam's strong, slow current catch the timbers and carry him away—away from the safety of his father's house, toward a wilderness that would never be tamed, a wilderness that nobody came home from. He watched his father and brothers get smaller in the growing distance. Then he raised his hand in a silent salute as they disappeared around the bend.

In the cool of the morning, scattered fog—the last of the night airs—lay in wisps on the surface of the water.

The trees along the riverside were loud with the songs of birds exulting in a new spring day. The forest bugs, too, were coming to life, tuning up the click and buzz that would grow slowly louder throughout the day and finally reach a crescendo in the hour before dark. The water was high with the spring rains and muddied a little more than usual, but the floods were past. It was perfect rafting water: high enough to submerge most of the logs and snags that might slow them but not high enough to sling them over the banks and into flooded swamps beyond.

Aidan discovered he had a natural talent for reading the river's current, and he assumed the role of pilot. The key to raft piloting, he discovered, was not reacting to the current's push but anticipating it—having the raft in position to manage every swirl, shoal, and eddy before it got there. He kept his two-man crew busy at their posts, but he stayed busier himself, running from bow to stern and back again to help whichever oarsman was pulling hardest at the moment.

They named their craft the *Headstrong,* for once it went in the wrong direction, it took the strength and perseverance of all three raftsmen to get it back on course. The greatest danger was the raft's tendency to drift out of the current. Sometimes, when the nose drifted toward the bank, the current would whip the back end around and send the raft into an uncontrolled spin. Other times, the raft might languish in the sluggish water near the river's edge, requiring great effort to get it moving again.

But when they did it right, the river did most of the work for them. Aidan soon learned to keep the

Headstrong in the swiftest current even in the river's sharpest, most treacherous turns. It was always tempting to pull into the slower water, to take what would seem the safer route and avoid the inevitable, bone-jarring slam of the stern on the high outside bank as it swung around in the current. But a river bend was no place for shrinking back. Aidan adopted the old rafters' cry as they shot into the river bends: "Keep to the current, boys, and let her slam!"

Even Massey and Floyd, it turned out, weren't bad at guiding a raft now that they could steer from either end. Under Aidan's guidance, the two alligator hunters were able to keep the raft booming along. The previous day's bickering over who should be captain disappeared. Everyone was too busy with his own tasks to worry about anyone else's.

For long stretches, the river was mostly straight and the raftsmen had little to do but talk and watch the river go by. For sheer joy of the river, Massey sang a rafting song he learned from timber rafters on the Eechihoolee River:

My sweet Eileen
Is the prettiest thing,
The ferry-keeper's daughter.
My heart's own queen
Is sweet Eileen,
She lives beside the water.

I gave Eileen
A ruby ring
To be my wife forever.

But she just sung,
"Boy, I'm too young!"
And threw it in the river.

So I departed
Brokenhearted,
Lonesome ever after.
I left the farm
And my mother's arms
To be a timber rafter.

Now every spring
I see Eileen
Beside the ferry landing.
I wave and sigh
As I float by,
And there I leave her standing.

My sweet Eileen
Is the prettiest thing,
The ferry-keeper's daughter.
My heart's own queen
Is sweet Eileen,
She lives beside the water.

Drifting by a willow bank the rafters saw a great blue heron, still as a statue, gazing fixedly at the water. It was watching for the shadows of fish beneath the water's murky surface. "Look at that craney-crow!" shouted Massey. Its concentration broken, the great blue-gray bird rose into the air with four slow, lumbering flaps of its wings, then tucked its long beak on its breast and glided along the surface of the water to a spot where it could have more privacy.

"When I was a boy," said Floyd, "there was a man in our village taught a craney-crow how to read."

"He never did!" answered Massey. "What do you mean he taught a craney-crow to read?"

"I mean you put some writing in front of that long-legged bird, and he could read it."

"You're telling me a bird could look at a paper and tell you what the writing said?" asked Massey, sure his hunting partner was putting him on.

"I didn't say the man taught a craney-crow to talk," answered Floyd. "I said he taught one how to read. He'd just read quiet to himself—didn't even have to move his lips like you do, Massey."

"Then how in tarnation," asked Massey, "could you know he was reading and not just looking?"

"He had a real wise and solemn look in his eye," said Floyd. "Just looking at him you could see he knew what he was about." Massey didn't seem convinced, but Floyd went on, "And if you wrote something nice, like 'Good day, Craney-Crow' or 'Your baby chicks is growing big and pretty,' he'd bob his head like this here, like he's agreeing with you." Floyd jutted his head in imitation of a heron's head bob. "But if you wrote something he disagreed with, or if he felt like you was insulting him, he'd cock his head like this here and just stare at you—wouldn't blink or nothing—just stare at you like he was astonished somebody'd say such a thing to a self-respecting craney-crow."

Massey had his doubts, but he dropped the subject when he noticed two round eye-knobs and a pair of horn-rimmed nostrils poking from the river, just out of the main current a short distance in front of the raft.

"Look a-here, Floyd!" he shouted, pointing excitedly.

Floyd rose to his feet. "I see him, Massey." Alligator hunting was one subject Massey and Floyd could always agree on. Massey started making a loop in the mooring rope at the near corner. "Man the bow oar," he ordered, and Floyd was glad to oblige. The nose of the raft was almost even with the alligator now, but it wasn't quite close enough for Massey to throw the lasso with any confidence.

"Pull, man!" cried Massey to his partner. "Swing the bow around toward the gator!" Floyd strained against the long oar-sweep, struggling to nudge the nose of the massive craft a few feet to the left.

"Floyd? Massey?" Aidan interrupted. "That's a bad idea."

But there was no talking to Floyd and Massey. They were alligator hunters first and last. Floyd had made progress moving the bow. Seeing that the raft was getting diagonal to the current, Aidan ran to the stern oar to straighten it. He leaned his full weight against the oar-sweep, but it was too late. By the time Massey was ready to throw his lasso, Floyd had pulled the raft's nose out of the current. The back of the raft, still very much in the current, swung around. The raft was completely cross-ways in the channel before Massey and Floyd noticed what they had done. They pulled at the bow with everything they had, but the raft was completely out of control.

They were still spinning when the *Headstrong* was swept into the Narrows. The river was swift there and twisted between high bluffs on either side. They were at the river's mercy, and the river didn't appear to be feeling very merciful that day. The stern of the raft got drawn into a swirl as it careened around the first part of the bend. The raft was in a hard spin now, and the back corner slammed into the embankment. Aidan had lost his grip on the stern oar, and the force of the collision threw him into the swirling water.

Chapter Nine

Bullbat Bay

loyd ran to the stern to throw Aidan a rope, but it was no use. The current spun him away and the rope fell short. By the time Aidan managed to outswim the swirl, the raft was a hundred strides away, and the alligator hunters were having no success controlling it. Aidan eased himself into the current in the hope he could gain on the raft and be pulled in on a mooring rope. The raft, after all, couldn't go faster than the current. But in the alligator-infested Tam, Aidan preferred not to be in the water any longer than he had to, and he was very relieved when he saw the raft beach itself on a sandbar.

Aidan floated on his back until he got within a rope's length of the raft. Massey pulled him in the rest of the way. The alligator hunters were thankful Aidan was unharmed, but they were also embarrassed that their foolishness had endangered him. They mumbled sheepish apologies, which Aidan readily accepted.

It wasn't the time to dwell on past mistakes. They had a big problem on their hands. It was hard enough to move a raft of timber when it was floating. But a raft of timber on the ground—there was no budging it. Each log was fifteen strides in length, and most were so thick Aidan could barely reach around them at the base. It would take a mule to drag even one. Here they had forty such logs skidded halfway up their length onto the sandbar.

Floyd scratched his head. Now that Aidan was safe and sound, the magnitude of their problem was starting to dawn on him. "How in the world are we going to get this raft off this bar?"

It didn't take long for the three rafters to realize they would have to float the raft if they hoped to move it. "The river's been dropping for three days now," observed Massey. "And if it keeps dropping, this raft'll be completely beached by tomorrow."

"Spring rains is mostly over," added Floyd. "River's headed back to its usual flow. Who knows when it might rise enough to float these logs."

They all agreed that their best option was to take the raft apart, roll the logs one by one into the river, and refasten them on the water. With the river current, it was really more than a three-man job and could take days.

"We need a bigger crew," observed Aidan. "But we're a long way from the nearest settlement."

"Last Camp's another thirty leagues down the river," Massey estimated, "and Longleaf's the nearest civilization in the other direction."

"Some hunters might have an overnight camp nearby," offered Floyd. "And the Overland Trail to Last Camp can't be more than a couple of leagues from the river. Maybe we can meet up with some hunters passing through who might help." Any hunter who found himself in the Eastern Wilderness should be happy to help get the raft to Big Bend. The timber, after all, was for a stockade to protect anyone who used Last Camp.

Aidan, Floyd, and Massey pushed through the willow bank and into the scrub beyond. It was hard going as they picked their way among thickets of black haw bush and needle palm. The hoorah bushes were thick, too, with their tiny yellow flowers.

"Aidan, I bet you don't know how the hoorah bush got its name, do you?" said Floyd.

"No, I don't," answered Aidan, "but I bet you're going to tell me."

"Sure," answered Floyd, holding a branch from a galberry bush so it wouldn't snap back and hit Aidan, "since you asked."

"Long time ago," began Floyd, "the sweat bees around here was just about to starve to death. Every time they went to get the nectar out of a flower, there'd be a big bumblebee's behind sticking out of it, crowding the sweat bees out of the action. And worse than that, the bumbles was bullyish about it. It wasn't no use for the little sweat bees to ask them nicely could they please have a turn. The big bumbles just waggled their head feelers at them and kind of growled.

"For awhile there," Floyd continued, "the sweat bees worked out a partnership with the lightning bugs. After the bumbles went to bed, the lightning bugs would light the way for the sweat bees to do their nectaring at night. They went halves on the honey.

"But that didn't last very long after the lightning bugs realized they didn't even like honey. Meantime, the sweat bees had got so grouchy from lack of sleep that they couldn't get along with their own selves, much less with the lightning bugs.

"Well, sir, the Lord looked down and had pity on the poor sweat bees. He caused a new bush to grow in the swamp. It had tiny little yellow flowers. Next morning when the bumbles went zooming off, they saw the new yellow flowers, and they thought they looked mighty toothsome. But the big bumblebees were too fat and broad to get at the nectar. They bumped and wiggled and growled and buzzed, but they couldn't get no more than their head feelers inside the little yellow flowers.

"But the little sweat bees, it was like they was made for the new flower and the flower for them. They'd march right into the front parlor and suck out the sweetest drop of nectar they ever tasted. The sweat bees were so happy to have a bush of their own, they made up a little song:

Hoorah, hoorah, hoorah,
Here's the bush for me.
Bumble grumble,

Roll and tumble,
You won't get a drop or crumble.
Hoorah, hoorah, hoorah,
Here's the bush for me.

"And ever since," concluded Floyd, "that yellow-flowered bush has been called the hoorah bush."

Aidan snapped off a sprig of hoorah bush and stuck it in Floyd's hair. "Hoorah, hoorah, hoorah!" he sang.

They were walking up a low sand hill now, and when they reached the top they could see a little more of the surrounding terrain. As Massey scanned the treetops, his face softened with relief and recognition; he was obviously getting his bearings. He pointed at a stand of tall cypresses that rose above the surrounding scrubby oaks. "There's Bullbat Bay," he announced. "We can't be more than a half league from the trail."

"That's Bullbat, all right," Floyd agreed. "Look at them big nests."

There were dozens of great stick nests in the treetops. Aidan could see it was a rookery for big birds of some sort. A buzzard came sailing into one of the treetops, then another. "Is it a buzzard rookery?" asked Aidan.

"No, not a buzzard rookery," answered Massey. He shot a narrow-eyed look of concern at Floyd. "It's an egret rookery."

When a trio of raucous crows came flapping and croaking from one of the nests, Massey and Floyd took off toward the bay. Aidan had to step quick to keep up with the hunters, who walked with long strides and swinging arms as if drawn to the big cypress stand, even though they dreaded what they expected to find there.

Well before they reached Bullbat Bay, they were hit with a stench that lay over the place like a fog. The high whine of swarming bluebottle flies announced this was a place of death and corruption. When they got to the bay, they found the floor littered with the white carcasses of egrets. Dozens of the dead birds hung tangled in the bushes, lay contorted on the spongy ground, or floated where the water pooled. Their heads, backs, and breasts had been stripped of the long showy plumes that had been their glory. There was nothing glorious about this rookery now, where the magnificent white birds returned to the black muck.

Even more gruesome was the scene in the treetops. Squawking egret chicks sat helpless and unprotected in their stick nests. They stretched out their pink beaks, desperate for a meal that would never come. The crows and buzzards that lit on their nests came not to feed the chicks but to feed themselves. A single egret mother stood in a single nest, vigilantly guarding her young. But she had no mate to gather food for them or to take a turn protecting the nest so she could hunt herself. She faced a grim choice: to see her offspring starve or to leave them vulnerable to the carrion birds while she went in search of food for them.

"Plume hunters," growled Floyd, and he spat on the ground in disgust.

Aidan stood in shock at such a scene of devastation. The sheer number of birds shot and left to rot was nauseating in itself. But the timing of the slaughter—during nesting season before the young egrets could fend for themselves—ensured that the colony would never recover. This rookery was gone for good.

Aidan could feel his eyes filling with tears. "Why nesting time?" he asked. Even a hunter who cared nothing for the Living God's creation should care enough about his own livelihood not to hunt his quarry to extinction.

"Nesting time's the only time a plume hunter shoots," answered Massey. His face was red with anger. "It's the only time the birds wear their wedding plumage."

"Every spring," explained Floyd, "them poor birds put on their wedding plumes. They marry up, fix a little house out of sticks, have a few babies." He smiled at the thought of the egrets' domestic happiness. "They're so proud and pretty."

"That's when the plume hunters come," said Massey. "Circle 'round a rookery like this one and shoot their crossbows into the treetops."

"Big birds make easy targets," Floyd added, "standing guard over their babies, as still as statues. And so brave and stupid, they won't fly away and leave their young'uns unprotected once the shooting starts."

Massey picked up the grim account. "Before long, their mates sail in from fish hunting and light on the nest to feed their babies. Plume hunters shoot them too."

What Aidan saw at Bullbat Bay was a sickening sign that things would never be the same in the Eastern Wilderness. And not just in the wilderness. He thought of

King Darrow and his paranoid rants and wondered if he would ever again be the king he had been as a young man—the king who seemed to have reawakened three years ago when he led the charge that defeated the invading Pyrthens. He thought of his own father, so changed in the months since the king had discarded him. He thought of the fine ladies and gentlemen of Tambluff, in their fine plumed hats who either didn't care or kept themselves ignorant of the devastation wrought in the Eastern Wilderness so they could follow the latest fashions.

Aidan felt sick, as if his stomach had been turned inside out. He stood silent for a moment with his traveling partners. There was nothing they could do here; the irreparable damage had been done. And they were in desperate need of extra hands to help refloat the raft.

"There's a footpath on the far side of the bay," said Massey at last. "It leads to the Overland Trail a quarter league from here."

They walked the path without speaking. *Things are changing in the wilderness,* thought Aidan. There were no written laws in the Eastern Wilderness. Or rather, there was no authority there to enforce any law. The nearest magistrate, in fact, was Aidan's father, all the way back at Longleaf. For the few people who ventured into the wilderness, the only law was a code of honor. No hunter took from the forest more than he needed—just enough to eat, to clothe himself, a few extra pelts or hides to trade for the things he couldn't make or find. Nobody aimed to get rich from the forest. If that's what people wanted, they would move to town or raise cattle or cotton. Settlers lived in the wilderness because they loved the wilderness, not because they wanted to tame it or to convert its resources into gold to line their buckskin pockets. The first law of the wilderness was to keep it wild.

Aidan was so lost in his own thoughts he paid no attention to the rhythmic squeaking he heard to the east. The forest, after all, was full of squeaks and chirps at all hours of the day and night. Floyd was the first to realize that these weren't the noises of frogs and birds. He stopped and cupped a hand to his ear. "Is that wagon wheels I hear?" Aidan and Massey stopped, too, and they heard the jangle of a mule harness. They ran the short distance to the trail. They couldn't see the wagon, but they could still hear it creaking northward toward civilization.

"Wait!" shouted Massey as they sprinted up the trail. They couldn't let these travelers get away; it might be days before anyone else came along this remote path. "Hold on!"

"Wait for us," called Floyd.

The creaking of wagon wheels stopped. The wagoner had obviously heard them. When Aidan, Massey, and Floyd came running around the next bend in the trail, they skidded to a stop, shocked to find four sunburned men in buckskin breeches standing behind a wagon and aiming crossbows at them. Their eyes had the blank look of men who knew what it was to pull the trigger on another man. But the really mesmerizing thing about the men was their enormous hair. It stood high on their heads and flipped back like great duck wings, plastered with potato starch on either side. It was the past year's fashionable hairstyle in Tambluff.

Aidan and his fellow travelers instinctively raised their arms and froze where they stood. The mule stamped at the sandy ground and jingled in his traces, and a rain frog *chirrripped* from a bush beside the trail, but there was no other sound in the tense moment.

A fifth man, tall with a curling mustache, leaned on the side of the wagon. He was obviously their leader. He had the biggest hair of all. His elbow rested on a burlap-wrapped bale, about the height and width of a small breakfast table. He squinted at Aidan, and his mouth twitched slightly beneath his bristling mustache, but he didn't say anything.

Massey's surprise soon gave way to indignation. "What is this?" he demanded. "Why are you pointing those things at us like we was enemies or criminals?"

The lead wagoner seemed satisfied that Aidan and company were unarmed. He gestured for his men to lower their weapons. "In the forrrest," he explained, addressing Massey, "you can't be too keerrrful." In the man's speech, Aidan noticed the rolling *r*'s of Corenwald's hill country dialect.

Floyd noticed it too. "You boys ain't from around here, are you?" he asked. He observed the shiny red of deep sunburn on their cheeks and noses, and the insect bites that dotted every inch of skin not covered in buckskin, and he couldn't resist a little dig. "Eastern

Wilderness can be pretty mean on a bunch of hill-scratchers."

One of the crossbowmen, taking offense, leveled his weapon at Floyd's chest, but his leader reined him in again. "I rrreckon we're plenty mean ourrr own selves," he said with a hint of menace.

Massey paid little attention to the stranger's remark. There were a lot of tough talkers in the Eastern Wilderness. Massey was pretty tough himself, and he hadn't given up hope that these strangers would be of assistance. "The reason we flagged you down," he said, "was because we need some help." The lead wagoner said nothing but merely stared at Massey. Massey carried on. "We was floating a raft of timber down the Tam to Last Camp and beached it on a sandbar. We'd be obliged if you could help us get it back into the water."

The mustachioed stranger paused before answering. "I don't rrreckon we can. We got to get wherrre we going."

Floyd and Massey were astonished. "That ain't how we do things in the wilderness!" spluttered Floyd. "We help each other out, carry each other's load. 'Cause one of these days you gonna need somebody's help."

"Well, as you pointed out alrrready," said the stranger, "we ain't from around herrre."

Massey was furious. It wasn't only the strangers' refusal to help that enraged him—after all, sometimes a person wasn't in a position to help—but their total disregard for the ways of the wilderness was infuriating. That's when he realized what Aidan had known when he first set eyes on the wagoners. These were plume hunters, probably the ones who cleaned out Bullbat Bay. The bale in the wagon, no doubt, was a bale of plumes.

"What's in the wagon?" asked Massey. He knew he was probably picking a fight, but he didn't care.

The wagoners stared him down. "It's a cotton bale," lied their leader. "We'rrre taking it to market."

Floyd laughed at the bold-faced lie. "You got a cotton patch in the woods somewhere?"

"Yeah," said the tall stranger. "That's rrright."

Massey pointed at the bale in the wagon. "Kind of little for a cotton bale, ain't it?"

"We ain't verrry good farmers," answered the lead wagoner. The crossbowmen smirked.

Massey's thick neck was bulging, and his face turned as red as the sunburned wagoners'. "You're a liar, stranger! I know that's a bale of bird plumes."

The four crossbowmen raised their weapons again and fingered the triggers. "That's rrright," sneered their leader. "What do you aim to do about it?"

Aidan could see that letting Massey and Floyd do the talking wasn't going to work. And they certainly weren't going to be able to fight their way out of this mess. Besides being outnumbered, he and the alligator hunters didn't have a weapon among them. He spoke for the first time since they had hailed the wagon. "Ahem," he gestured at the lead plume hunter. "Could I have a word?" He gave a broad, knowing wink. The plume hunter waved him over, and they stepped off the trail while the rest of the plume hunters continued to hold Floyd and Massey at arrowpoint.

Aidan spoke in a low, conspiratorial tone. "My friends here are a little old-fashioned. Not what you'd call men of the world. But they're harmless."

The stranger didn't react, but he seemed to be listening. Aidan continued: "The way I look at it, if folks in Tambluff—or Pyrth, even—want plumes, they're going to get plumes. They might as well get them from you. Am I right?" The stranger raised his eyebrows. He was warming up just a little.

"Here's the thing," said Aidan, leaning in a little closer. "I know a man who'd be very interested in your plumes."

"I've alrrready got a buyer," answered the plume hunter.

"Where's your buyer?" asked Aidan. "Tambluff? Middenmarsh?" The stranger didn't answer. Aidan was undeterred. "That's a long way to haul such a valuable load." He pointed at the armed men who were menacing his friends. "It's a long time to pay four guards." He paused dramatically. "I know a man at the edge of the wilderness."

"I'm listening," said the stranger. He was calculating what the saved travel days would mean to him.

"Follow this trail to its end at the River Road." Aidan was whispering now. "Turn north on the River Road, and the first farmstead you come to is called Longleaf. Ask for Errol."

"This Errol," asked the plume hunter, "does he pay market price?"

"He'll give you exactly what's due you," Aidan assured him.

"'Cause plume hunting ain't easy," said the hunter, "and I aim to collect what I've got coming to me."

"Don't you worry about that," said Aidan. "Errol will give you everything you've got coming to you." He found it hard not to smile at the thought of his father giving these rogues what they deserved. That would put a spring back in the old boy's step. Aidan only wished he could be there to see it.

"Tell you what," said Aidan. "You call your guards off my friends there, and I'll even write you a letter to hand to Errol when you get there."

The plume hunter thought a moment, then shrugged his shoulders. "Why not?" he said. He motioned to the crossbowmen again, and again they pointed their weapons at the ground. The tall stranger looked under the seat of the wagon and found a sheet of palmetto paper, an inkpot, and a quill pen made from an egret plume, gaudily fluffy and as long as Aidan's forearm. Such a dandyish writing instrument seemed comically out of place in the wilderness, but the plume hunter seemed proud of it. Aidan nodded in mock appreciation and began writing:

Dear Errol—

The bearer of this letter and his four companions are plume hunters I met in the Eastern

Wilderness. As we recently discussed, I trust you will take real pleasure in dealing with them.

Yours sincerely,
Aidan

‡ ‡ ‡

Standing with Massey and Floyd, Aidan waved to the plume hunters as their wagon disappeared down the trail.

"What was that all about?" asked Massey when the wagon was gone.

"Boys," answered Aidan, "today wasn't the day for us to take care of those lying, thieving, no-account, big-haired poachers. But I sent them to somebody who will." The alligator hunters looked quizzically at him. "Remember yesterday when Father said he'd like to get his hands on a few plume hunters?" They nodded their heads. "He's about to get his chance."

Aidan glanced to the northwest, back toward Longleaf, wondering what would happen to the plume hunters when they got there. That's when he noticed darkening clouds in the west. Lightning split the sky, followed by rumbling thunder. He pointed at the approaching storm. "That might be the help we need!"

The rain started before they got to Bullbat Bay. It was a frog-strangler, with big, heavy drops driving down, whipped into the men's faces by an angry wind. It was the kind of rain that could raise the level of the river a few inches if it could keep it up long enough, or if it rained enough along the creeks that fed the river upstream from the raft. And all they needed were a few extra inches of water.

By the time they got back to the sandbar, the river had risen enough that the *Headstrong*, though not yet clear of the sand, was starting to sway a little in the water. The raft's crew stood on the sandbar, exposed to the lashing wind and rain, cringing at the earth-shaking thunder and rejoicing in the power of a creation that could lift a hundred-ton raft of logs and place it back on its path. When the rising Tam freed the *Headstrong*, Massey, Floyd, and Aidan were on it, eager to continue their voyage to Last Camp.

By the time the rain stopped, Aidan was having second thoughts about sending five armed and dangerous plume hunters to his father's house. He pulled a sheet of palmetto paper out of his pack and cut a narrow strip. He wrote a brief message to his father.

> *Five plume hunters coming your way. Armed.*
> *Be ready. Aidan.*

He wrapped the message around the leg of Jasper's homing pigeon with a piece of twine and let the bird go.

Watching the pigeon dart upriver toward Longleaf, Aidan felt good about the old warrior's chances against the five unsuspecting plume hunters. Errol had no shortage of strong men to call on for such occasions. More to the point, as official magistrate of Hustingshire and the Eastern Wilderness, Errol had the authority to deal with criminals in those regions. Aidan felt sure it would revive his father's spirits to administer a bit of frontier justice on the very people who represented the demise of the wild Corenwald he knew so well. Aidan turned his face back toward Last Camp and smiled.

Chapter Ten

Last Camp

he whole population of Last Camp—six hunters, a camp cook, and fourteen very eager hunting dogs— was waiting at the landing when the *Headstrong* nosed into the bank. It was nearly dark, three days since the raft had left Longleaf and more than two weeks since the men at Last Camp had seen Floyd and Massey. Amid much hooting, back slapping, and coonskin cap tossing, the three raftsmen stepped ashore with the swaggering confidence of real rafthands.

"Here's your stockade, boys," announced Floyd. And because he could never resist tweaking Cooky, he added, "Now, where's my supper?"

"I thought you was drownded," grumbled the crusty old cook, his wiry gray beard wagging. "It's bad enough you two coming back alive right before supper," he waved his ladle toward Aidan, "without you bringing an extry mouth for me to feed."

Aidan couldn't help but smile at Cooky's exaggerated gruffness as the old man stumped back to his cooking fire. "I won't eat much," he called after him. "And I won't stay long."

Floyd presented Aidan to the group. "Boys," he said, "this is Aidan Errolson from Longleaf. Aidan, this here's Burl, Chaney, Big Haze, Little Haze, Isom, and Hugh. You already met Cooky."

Aidan shook hands with each of the men, repeating each name to be sure he had it right. He liked these men already. They were weather-toughened and strong of limb, and in their broad, open faces he saw a confidence that allowed them to be genuinely welcoming of the stranger in their midst.

"I know you," said Big Haze. "You're the boy killed that giant."

"Well," answered Aidan, "he wasn't actually a giant."

"If he weren't a giant, he was something mighty like a giant," interrupted Massey. "Anyway, Haze, you got it right. This is the same Aidan Errolson. I seen him handle five plume hunters too."

"With at least four crossbows between them," added Floyd. "And he ain't a half-bad raft pilot neither."

"Hey, Cooky," called Burl, "I hope your supper's better'n usual tonight. We got a sure-enough hero amongst us."

Cooky scowled over his stew pot. "Any hero don't like my cooking can fix his own supper. That goes for flea-bit deer hunters too."

There were no permanent buildings at Last Camp. The stockade, when built from the logs they brought, would be the first. There were four or five wagons, including Cooky's covered mess wagon, and several deer-skin tents encircled the fire. But there were more empty tent sites than there were tents. Last Camp usually bustled with at least twenty hunters—more in the autumn—but the place was nearly deserted now.

"Where is everybody?" asked Floyd. But he suspected he knew the answer.

"Culler and Minty are hunting deer over at Longpond," said Burl. "They're camping up there tonight. But everybody else has quit us."

"Hadley and Munce said they wanted to try farming," offered Hugh, "and Redden went back up north to the mines."

"Folks just sort of drifted off," Little Haze added. "Wiley went to work with his uncle, who's a butcher in Tambluff. He figured that was better work than getting shot at every night."

"It's got worse since you left," explained Burl. "Most nights now we're getting attacked. Nobody's got hurt or killed yet. Whoever's shooting up the camp just wants to scare us."

"They doing a thorough job of that," said Isom. "All that hollering in the trees scares me as bad as the arrows and spears." He gave a little shudder. "Makes my blood cold."

"I want to start on that stockade at first light tomorrow," said Chaney. "It won't be long before some of them arrows or spears hurts somebody, whether they're trying to or not."

By time time, Cooky was ladling up supper, a stew made of rabbit and possum. Aidan ate his hungrily, and his genuine enjoyment of the meal softened Cooky toward him. The campfire conversation was lively. Massey and Floyd gave a full account of their river adventure—from their near destruction of the Hustingreen waterfront to their run-in with the plume hunters.

But Aidan, of course, was the main attraction. Except for Little Haze, who hadn't been fighting age at the time of the last Pyrthen invasion, all of the hunters had been at the Battle of Bonifay, attached to the same infantry company. Even Cooky was there, serving as their mess sergeant. So they had all witnessed Aidan's combat with Greidawl. They eagerly relived the day of Corenwald's greatest victory—the reawakening of a valor that had nearly dwindled away, the terror of the Pyrthen thunder-tubes, the exhilaration of the last charge across the plain that drove the invaders from the island. They insisted on hearing the details of Aidan's trek through the caverns under the battlefield and the climactic explosion of the Pyrthen flame powder that set the rout in motion.

Talk turned inevitably to the strange happenings in the Eechihoolee Forest. "The best part of the whole thing," said Burl eagerly, "was after we run the Pyrthens into the swamp, and they come running back to surrender." He chuckled at the thought of the Pyrthens' panic-stricken faces as they tripped over one another to be the first to hand themselves over to the enemy.

"After a quarter hour in the Eechihoolee, those old boys weren't looking so proud and shiny," added Floyd. "Their faces was as ashy as a possum's. And their eyes was like this." He held two disks of sweet potatoes to his eyes to imitate the Pyrthens' bulging eyes. He ran around the circle of the fire, still holding the sweet potatoes to his eyes. "Help me!" he shouted in an exaggerated Pyrthen accent. "Save me from the lizard people! Save me from the tree alligators!" But the sweet potatoes obstructed his view, and he tripped over a chunk of firewood, much to the amusement of the others.

"What chapped my hide," said Burl, "was the way our own officers tried to explain everything away. Said it was just crazy talk, said the Pyrthens was seeing things that wasn't there."

"Ain't that just like town folks and hill-scratchers?" Massey interjected. "Anybody who's spent any time out east here knows different. I've seen a lizard man my own self."

"I've seen one too," offered Chaney.

"We've all seen 'em," Isom added.

"Sometimes you look across the river there," said Burl. He pointed to the south bank of the Tam. "And them trees is just alive, just crawling."

"Crawling with what?" asked Aidan.

"I don't know exactly," answered Burl. "But all that hollering and hooting we heard that day in the Eechihoolee right before the Pyrthens come running back out, that wasn't the only time any of us Last Campers ever heard it."

"It's a long way from here to Tambluff," said Massey. "In Tambluff, you can go for days and never have dirt underneath your boots, only cobblestones. You can tip your high-plumed hat at a lady on the street and neither of you think about how that plume got from a bird's back to your head. You can watch the alligators lazying in the castle moat and pretend you've faced the beast. In Tambluff, you can believe we've got the whole creation under our control. Seems strange to me that the folks who make the decisions for this whole kingdom live in such a place as that."

"But out here," said Isom, "the nursery tales of feechiefolk and the Wilderking don't seem all that fantastic—no stranger than the world that buzzes just across the river and in the forests all around us."

Big Haze looked across the fire at Aidan. "You're sitting at the edge of the world, Aidan. How does it feel?"

Aidan smiled. "I like it here. It feels more like home than Tambluff Castle."

The hunters cheered and laughed, flattered by Aidan's remark. Tambluffers were a rarity at Last Camp, and even rarer were Tambluffers who accepted the hunters on their own terms.

"Well, if you don't mind my asking," said Burl, "what brings you to Last Camp?"

Aidan measured his words. "I'm out here to fetch something for King Darrow."

"You ain't the tax man, are you?" asked Cooky.

"No," Aidan assured him and laughed.

"So what have you come to fetch?" pressed Chaney.

"Ain't no use asking," Floyd interrupted. "Me and Massey had him surrounded three days on a raft, and we never got it out of him."

Before anyone had a chance to ask another question, the forest erupted in a series of blood-curdling cries: "*Haaa-wwwweeeeee! Haaa-wwwweeeeee! Haaa-wwwweeeeee!*" The hunters dove to the ground and tucked themselves into tight balls in order to make smaller targets for the arrows that came whistling into the camp. Half a dozen arrows embedded themselves with a *thwack* in the logs where the hunters had been sitting. Another arrow glanced off Cooky's stew pot, ringing it like a bell and careening into the forest on the other side of the camp. A spear stuck in the ground less than two feet from Aidan's boots.

"Aidan! Get down!" shouted Massey. "It ain't over yet!"

But Aidan didn't get down. Among all the people at Last Camp, only he understood exactly what the forest hollers were: feechie battle cries. And he felt he could do something to stop the attack. He grabbed a small log that was half in the fire and brandished it for a torch, trying to catch the gleam of feechie eyes in the forest. Then, even as arrows continued to sail into the camp, he belted out a blood-curdling yell of his own: "*Ha-ha-ha-hrawffff-wooooooooo . . . Ha-ha-ha-hrawffff-woooooooooo.*"

The woods grew still as the echoes of Aidan's watch-out bark subsided. Aidan thought he heard the slightest rustle in the treetops—a rustle that grew more distant as the attackers receded into the forest. Still bearing the torch, Aidan ventured a few steps beyond the camp into the trees, as if in pursuit of the attackers. But they were gone.

"What just happened?" asked Floyd. He was looking at Aidan with undisguised awe.

"What was that holler you just did?" asked Isom, equally amazed.

"It sounded," gasped Chaney, "like the bark of the bog owl."

But Aidan didn't hear them. He was inspecting one of the short, white-feathered arrows the feechies had shot into the camp. "Who fletches an arrow with egret feathers?" he asked aloud. And the arrowhead was equally perplexing. It was made of burnished steel.

Chapter Eleven

Beyond the Tam

edroll, hardtack, water bladder, alligator jerky, tinder box . . ." Rocking with the flow of the River Tam and the push and pull of Massey's oar strokes, Aidan took one last inventory of his backpack's contents. He felt for the hunting knife at his belt and counted the arrows in his quiver.

"I don't like this one bit, Aidan," said Massey as he leaned back on the oars, propelling the little skiff across the water. "Not one bit."

"I know you don't," answered Aidan, "but if you don't row me over, I'll just swim across."

"And get et up by gators," Massey grumbled. "Which, for all I know, ain't no worse'n what's going to happen to you once I've handed you over to the swamp critters on the south bank." He nodded back toward Last Camp. "There's a reason we call it Last Camp. It's because you can't go no further. Because when folks go past it, it's the last time you ever hear from 'em." He was hurt that Aidan had waited until this morning—the very morning of his departure—to mention he was crossing the river. Three days on the raft together— three days Massey could have had to talk the boy out of this foolishness—but he had waited until this morning to spring it on him. And Aidan still hadn't revealed the real nature of his mission.

"King Darrow sent me across the river," said Aidan matter-of-factly. "And I'm going across the river."

Massey grunted but said no more. Neither of them spoke for the remainder of the crossing. The river was broader here than it was at Longleaf, and deeper, too, swelled by the waters of countless creeks and smaller rivers that joined the Tam along its twisting course.

When the little boat nosed into the high bank on the other side, Massey tied up to a root tangle, clambered to level ground, and reached a hand down to pull up Aidan and his gear. The old alligator hunter looked at the moss-hung trees and shuddered. "I ain't never been on this side of the river," he remarked.

"Looks a lot like the other side, don't you think?" answered Aidan, shrugging into his backpack.

"Aidan," said Massey suddenly, "Darrow ain't king of Feechiefen."

Aidan smiled at Massey. "Darrow may not be king of Feechiefen, but he's king of Aidan Errolson, whether I'm at his table or out here past the edge of civilization."

Massey nodded. He wouldn't try again to talk Aidan out of his foolish mission, whatever it was. "You better get going then," he said. He embraced Aidan awkwardly, patting his backpack with a hamlike hand. Then, not really knowing what else to say, he added, "We sure showed them plume hunters, didn't we, Aidan?"

"We sure did, Massey."

Massey turned and strode quickly toward the river. But before the old alligator hunter disappeared down the steep bank, Aidan thought he saw him swipe at his eyes with a hairy hand. "Thanks, Massey!" he called after him, but Massey made no answer.

Aidan was alone now. Very alone. He stood on the far side of the River Tam, where even the rough customers of Last Camp never dared come. He told himself what he had told Massey: Things looked the same on the south side of the river as they did on the north side. The same birds *thirrruped* in the same gum trees and sweet bays. The same lizards skittered across the same palmetto fans. The same thick-bodied cottonmouth snakes left the same meandering tracks in the sticky mud beside the wet places.

But every step took him away from the familiarity of the river, from the comforts of the hunters' comradeship. Every step made it harder to convince himself that things weren't so very different on this side of the river. Every treetop rustle became ominous, a prelude to another attack like the previous night's barrage on Last Camp. Every movement in the bushes made him think of a feechie ambush.

"No," he said aloud in an effort to calm his own fears. Real feechies wouldn't make any noise in the treetops, and they surely wouldn't let themselves be seen if they were setting an ambush. But that realization did little to comfort Aidan, for now he was spooked by trees that *didn't* rustle, by bushes that *didn't* move. And every step took him closer to Feechiefen Swamp, from which no one had ever returned.

It took Aidan nearly an hour to push through the dense, vine-tangled forest of the bottomlands. But when he reached the edge of the floodplain, a gain of just a few feet in elevation produced a whole new landscape. The density of the swamp scrub gave way to the shaggy openness of a vast pine savanna. The land was as flat as the open plains. And, as on the open plains, the high grasses rippled and shimmered with every shifting breeze. But there was no mistaking this place for open plain. This was a forest, populated by massive, high-canopied pine trees with long, drooping needles that sighed softly when the breeze played through them. These were the longleaf pines for which Errol's estate was named, and being among them made Aidan feel as if he were home again.

The trees offered a dappled, shifting shade to the trav-eler while leaving plenty of space in the understory for the breezes not found in the swamp. Though not as dense as the river-bottom forest, these woods were no less alive. Great black-masked fox squirrels, the size of small dogs, dashed along the lower limbs as Aidan made his way through the forest. Enormous red-plumed woodpeckers, as big as crows, sailed high over Aidan's head to hammer away at dead branches where bugs were most abundant. The claw marks by which bears marked their territory marred the trunks of many trees.

The ground in the pine flats was pocked with the holes of gopher tortoises, big, lumbering, high-shelled tortoises that burrowed underground to live. The burrows would have been a hazard to a horse, had Aidan been riding one. A foot or so across, these black holes leading to a subterranean coolness stood in stark contrast to the bright, hot sand from which they were dug.

Here, out of the humid greenness of the floodplain, the light was different—clear, bright, intense where it stabbed between the needles of the pine trees. Aidan decided to make himself a sun hat. He cut two palmetto fans and wove their fronds together to make a peaked cap. He left the stem on one of the palm fans and let it trail along behind—a stiff and prickly plume, a nod to the Tambluffer fashion in hats.

Aidan whistled a merry tune as he trekked through the forest. He felt better able to think now that he was out of the ominous tangle of Tamside Forest. He couldn't explain the irrational fear of feechies that had overtaken him before. His whole mission depended on his connecting with feechies. He couldn't find King Darrow's frog orchid without guidance from the feechies who lived in the swamp. Besides, he knew many feechies and liked them. And all the feechies he had ever met liked him too. At least, they liked him eventually, after he had broken through their natural suspicion of civilizers. He glanced down at the alligator-shaped scar Chief Gergo had seared into his right forearm. He bore the feechiemark. Any feechie he met was bound by the Feechie Code to be a friend to him.

But still, he was in the feechies' world now, and he didn't know whether the rules might be different here.

Before, the feechies he had met were just passing through. They were at the edge of his world. But he was beyond Last Camp now, where feechies were in charge of things, where civilizers weren't welcome. Even if Chief Gergo's band was glad to see him—and even that wasn't a given— what about the other bands of feechies who populated the vast Feechiefen? Would they all honor Chief Gergo's feechiemark?

Aidan couldn't stop thinking about the previous night's attack on Last Camp. It was the work of feechies; it had to be. They shot from the treetops and escaped through the treetops. What civilizer could do that? And the feechie battle cries sounded authentic to him. But on the other hand, those weren't feechie arrows that were shot into the camp. They were steel-tipped. Aidan knew from Dobro that feechies didn't work with metal; not that they couldn't, but that they wouldn't. They thought it was cheating to use cold-shiny weapons, to use any materials they couldn't find in the swamp or in the river- bottom forests where they traveled.

Then there was the matter of the egret feathers. Arrow fletchers used whatever feathers were most readily avail- able to them. Every arrow Aidan had ever seen was fletched with the wing feathers from ducks or geese, sometimes chickens—barnyard birds, not forest birds. What civilizer—for Aidan was convinced the arrows were made by civilizers, even if they were shot by feechies—would find it easier to get egret feathers than duck or goose feathers?

The question had just begun to form in Aidan's mind

when a sudden dry buzzing near his feet drove out all conscious thought and replaced it with unthinking fear. It was a rattlesnake coiled on the sandy apron of a tortoise hole. Aidan stopped in his tracks, afraid even to step backward for fear the movement would incite the great snake to strike. The grinning snake wagged its head a foot above its heaping coils and fixed Aidan with its black eyes. It meant to strike.

Moving slowly but as smoothly as he could, never breaking eye contact with the snake, Aidan reached behind him and slipped his palmetto hat off the back of his head. Gripping the stem that he had left on the palm fan, he slowly, fluidly extended his right arm to its full length, the hat a foot or so beyond that. The snake had thought to mesmerize Aidan with its slitted, unblinking eyes. But now it was Aidan who held the snake enthralled. The snake flicked its tongue and continued waving back and forth, tenser and tauter with every touchy second.

Then, with the least twitch of his wrist, Aidan rattled the palmetto hat. Jarred out of its spell, the snake lunged for the big, bristling target. The force of the flying snake knocked the palm fans out of Aidan's hand as violently as a blow from a club.

Laid out to its full length, the snake was at its most vulnerable. Aidan's boot plunged down on the snake's head before it could recoil for another strike. Aidan felt the snake's head crack beneath his boot. Its tail whipped up and the writhing body twisted around his legs. But the rattlesnake was dead.

When Aidan held the snake's crushed head at shoulder height, its rattles—nine of them—dragged the ground. Aidan was amazed at how heavy it was. But then again, it was as big around as Aidan's calf and five feet long; it ought to be heavy.

When his heartbeat finally subsided to something like its normal rate, it occurred to Aidan that he was hungry. It was well past noon. Aidan looked at the huge snake. Father had always frowned on killing an animal one didn't plan to eat. He didn't see how he could eat that much snake meat, but he might as well eat what he could and save what little smoked alligator jerky he had in his backpack.

Using deadfall branches and the previous year's dry pine straw, Aidan got a fire started in a patch of thick sand where no grass grew. While the fire grew to cooking heat, he skinned the rattlesnake and cut it into chunks that could be skewered on small branches and roasted over the fire.

It wasn't long before the smells of roasting snake meat began to waft up from the fire. Aidan closed his eyes, savoring the smell, growing hungrier by the moment.

But Aidan wasn't the only one in the forest who was tantalized by the sizzling snake meat. When Aidan opened his eyes, he saw three red wolves, attracted by the smoky aroma, stalking a tightening spiral around him, one slow step at a time. They slunk with heads lowered, reddish fur bristling on their high-jutting shoulder blades. Foaming slobber dripped from their teeth and curling lips, and their yellow eyes were locked intently on Aidan. They appeared to be under the impression that Aidan was giving off the mouth-watering, irresistible smells that had attracted them.

Aidan fumbled for his bow and arrow leaning on the backpack beside him. He notched an arrow to the string, knowing he couldn't drop more than one of the approaching wolves, but praying that the other two would run away if he did. He pointed his arrow at the closest wolf, a mere twenty strides away. But even as he did, he could feel the wolf behind him come on a little more quickly. He wheeled around to face that wolf, exposing his back to the first wolf. He wheeled again. Three wolves, one arrow; he was bewildered. Aidan's indecision made matters worse. All three wolves were coming faster now. He could see the pink of their tongues.

Aidan was about to let fly with his arrow when the forest around him exploded in shouts.

"You stay away from my snake meat, you red-fur varmints!"

"That's my supper, you mangy pine-dogs!"

"Haaa-wwwweeeeee!"

Distracted from Aidan, the wolves looked over their shoulders, but before they could react, they were set upon by three he-feechies who appeared from behind trees. Each grabbed a wolf by its bushy tail and slung it into the woods. The wolves ran yelping into the forest.

Aidan stood with his hand over his heart. "Hallelujah!" he gasped. "You saved me! And just in the nick of time."

"Saved you?" snorted the biggest of the feechies, the one wearing a bear-claw necklace. "Hek, hek, hek, you ain't saved, civilizer."

"Naw," said the short one. "Your troubles is just getting started good."

Chapter Twelve

A Wrestling Match

Y ou think we'd risk life and liver to save a civilizer from a pack of wolves?" chuckled the biggest feechie. He seemed genuinely amused at the idea. "But roasted snake meat, that's something worth saving."

"Mmmmm," the third he-feechie chimed in dreamily, "I do love roasted snake meat."

The short feechie spoke. "We was going to leave you to mix it with them wolves, for the sport of it, you know." He smiled good-naturedly as he said it; it obviously didn't occur to him that Aidan may not see the sport in being torn to bits by wolves. "But we was afraid that if we did that, the wolves might get to the snake meat before we could."

"Mmmmm," repeated the third feechie, "I do love roasted snake meat."

"Now, give me my snake meat," snarled the bear-claw feechie. He pushed roughly past Aidan and snatched a skewer off the fire.

"Hold on there," said Aidan, indignantly. "I've got more than enough for everybody, and I'm glad to share, but I don't like being talked to that way."

"Humph!" grunted the feechie as he pinched off a piece of sizzling meat and thumbed it into his mouth. "Ain't your snake meat to share. It's mine. And I don't believe I'm gonna share any with you."

"It's not your snake!" Aidan's voice was rising both in volume and pitch.

The feechie clinched his fists and stuck out his chin in a posture of challenge. "You calling me a liar?" he growled.

Aidan's eyes flashed as he answered the feechie's belligerent tone. "I killed this snake. I skinned it. I cooked it."

The bear-claw feechie looked toward the short one. "You heard that, didn't you, Orlo? This civilizer just admitted to killing, skinning, and cooking *my* rattlesnake."

Aidan stared at the he-feechie and shook his head. "That's ridiculous," he muttered.

Aidan's challenger brightened considerably at this remark. "You heard that, Pobo?" he said excitedly to the third feechie. "I'm ridicaliss."

"You're ridicaliss, all right," answered Pobo. Then he thought for a moment. "What's a ridicaliss?"

"Well, I don't exactly know," answered Bear Claws. "But it's a awful rude thing to call another person." He looked to Orlo for confirmation.

Orlo obliged. "No question about it, Hyko. This civilizer has insulted you something terrible." He shook his head, shocked at Aidan's rudeness. "To stand right there and call a man a ridicaliss right to his face!" He made a clucking sound of disapproval. "The rudeswap is done. Hyko, you got no choice but to fight him."

"Hee-haw!" shouted the exultant Hyko. He balled his spidery fingers into hard fists and whirled them around like a windmill. Orlo and Pobo whooped and waved their arms and egged Hyko on.

"Eat him up, Hyko!"

"Skin him out!"

"You show that civilizer what a ridicaliss can do!"

Aidan sighed. He really didn't have time for a feechie fight, but he saw that there would be no way out of it. He had been tricked into a rudeswap, and the feechies would see it to its conclusion. Hyko swirled around him in ever smaller circles, waiting for Aidan to present his fists. Aidan thought it best to use an old favorite method of the feechies: surprise. Rather than raising his fists, he lowered his head and rammed Hyko right below the breastbone, like an angry billy goat.

Hyko went down on his back, the wind knocked out of him. Orlo and Pobo fell silent, astonished that a civilizer could be getting the better of a feechie in a free fight. Before Hyko could recover, Aidan was on top of him. He grabbed the feechie by the long hair at the nape of his neck and ground his forehead into the sand.

Orlo and Pobo were back at it now, screaming encouragement to their fellow feechie.

"Don't let a civilizer whup you, Hyko!"

"What would your mama say if she saw you beat by a civilizer?"

"Think of your mama, Hyko!"

Their words of encouragement—plus the fact that Hyko had finally gotten his breath back—revived him. He caught Aidan's left thumb in his mouth and bit down at the first knuckle. Aidan cut loose with an anguished scream that set a covey of quail burring from a nearby galberry bush. Afraid that the feechie would bite his thumb off, Aidan reached his free hand over the top of Hyko's head and hooked a finger into each of his nostrils. Then he yanked back for all he was worth. Hyko opened his mouth to scream with pain and rage, and Aidan was able to pull his thumb free.

Hyko writhed on the ground, holding his nose, and Aidan held his swelling thumb, praying that the feechie fight was over. But Hyko answered the call of his shouting comrades and rose again to come after Aidan. Aidan raised his fists to be ready for him.

"Hold on! Hold on! Hold on!" The high, grating voice of Pobo interrupted the combat. He was staring at Aidan. When he walked over and grabbed Aidan by the arm, Aidan tried to jerk away, afraid that he was about to have to take on all three feechies at once. But Pobo wouldn't let him go. With his finger he traced the alligator-shaped burn scar on Aidan's forearm. "This civilizer's got a feechiemark," announced Pobo. "He's a feechiefriend!"

"A feechiefriend?" exclaimed Hyko. "Why didn't you say so?" He rubbed his nose. "Might have saved me a nose ache."

Pobo asked, "What's your name, friend?"

"It's Aidan, Aidan Errolson of Longleaf Manor."

"Well, I'm Pobo Sands. This is Orlo Sands, and the feller what's been gnawing on your thumb is Hyko Vinesturgeon." The three feechies butted heads with Aidan by way of greeting, then Aidan said, "Pobo Sands, Orlo Sands—are you brothers?" Both Sandses looked down at their bare toes and shook their heads. "Cousins?" asked Aidan. Still looking at the sand, they shook their heads again. Aidan realized he had touched a sore subject.

Hyko quickly intervened. "Aidan," he said, "how 'bout you tell us how you come by that feechiemark?"

"Chief Gergo gave it to me," he answered. "In Bayberry Swamp."

"Gergo . . . Gergo . . ." Orlo was trying to put a face with the name. "He the one-legged feller with the scar across his forehead?"

"Naw," answered Hyko. "That's Chief Pardo you thinking about. Gergo's the one missing two fingers and a eye. I got a cousin in Gergo's band. Name's Theto Elbogator."

"Sure," said Aidan. "I remember him."

"So what'd you do to get made a feechiefriend," asked Orlo, "instead of, you know, getting fed to alligators?"

Aidan laughed. "It was because I killed a panther, saved the life of a fellow named Dobro Turtlebane."

"Ahhhhhww!" all three feechies gasped in recognition. Their eyes, previously narrowed in suspicion, now shone with awe. "You the one what's called Pantherbane, ain't you?" asked Hyko.

"That's right," answered Aidan. "That's the feechie name Chief Gergo gave me, since I killed a panther."

"Everybody in Feechiefen knows about Pantherbane," explained Pobo, growing more excited. "How he kilt a panther with a rock slinger and grabbled a catfish bigger than he was . . ."

Ever modest, Aidan clarified: "It wasn't *that* big!"

"He won the gator grabble the first time he ever tried it," added Orlo. Both feechies spoke of him as if he weren't right there.

"It was because of Pantherbane that we got to hide in the Eechihoolee Forest and scare off them foreigner civilizers with the black shirts made outta cold-shiny."

"I don't reckon I've had more fun than that in all my born days," said Orlo. He smiled, remembering the terrified Pyrthens crashing through the forest, bouncing off trees, and falling over roots to escape the feechie ambush. Orlo quoted the feechiefriend ceremony: "His fights is our fights, and our fights is his'n."

Hyko touched his nose with reverence. "Pantherbane hisself nearbout tore my nose off!"

"Say, Hyko, that reminds me," said Pobo. "You and Pantherbane ain't finished with your fight yet."

"Awww, Pobo," groaned Hyko, "I ain't so interested in fighting him now that he's Pantherbane."

"Don't start that foolishness," shot back Orlo. "You know the rules. You boys has swapped rude. It ain't over till somebody's whupped." Neither Orlo nor Pobo was willing to be cheated out of a chance to watch a first-rate fistfight.

"Well, how 'bout we just have a rassling match?" suggested Hyko. Pobo and Orlo reluctantly agreed, and Aidan, questioning the need for such strict and unbending rules regarding rudeswaps and fistfights and wrestling matches, squared off again against the feechie with the bear-claw necklace.

Orlo laid the ground rules for the match. Actually, there weren't really any rules, except that the winner would be the first to pin his opponent's shoulders to the ground for a count of three. At the last minute, however, Pobo thought of a new rule, a second way to win the match: If either competitor could stuff his opponent's head into a tortoise burrow, he would be declared the winner.

The combatants locked up for the start of their match, face to face, arm on arm, hands on one another's shoulders. They circled one another once, then twice, looking for any advantage to press. Aidan was much bigger than Hyko, even though Hyko was quite big for a feechie, but Aidan knew better than to put too much stock in a size advantage. Feechies could whip a bigger man out of pure caginess and meanness, and they were much stronger than they looked.

"Stop dancing and start rassling," called Orlo, who had been named the referee.

"You look just like a couple of civilizers," jeered Pobo, but he looked a little sheepish when Orlo elbowed him and reminded him that one of the wrestlers *was* a civilizer.

Hyko made the first move. He lunged to butt Aidan on the bridge of the nose. But Aidan was too quick. He bobbed his head out of the way, then lurched backward, pulling the off-balance Hyko on top of him. He grabbed the wiry feechie and easily twisted him in a knot. It was Aidan's signature move, the one with which he had won the kingdomwide wrestling tournament. Hyko's arms and legs were bent back in a contortion that had always caused Aidan's opponents to surrender in tears. But Hyko was so limber, he seemed not to be bothered in the least. Aidan clamped down harder, determined to break the feechie's stubbornness. But Hyko paid him little mind. In fact, the strain of the difficult hold seemed to be greater on Aidan than on his supposed victim. His forehead glistened with sweat, and his grip grew slippery. Hyko, on the other hand, actually smiled as Aidan wrenched his limbs into ever more strenuous contortions.

Aidan hoped Hyko was about to beg for mercy when the feechie twisted his head around so that his nose was a mere inch from Aidan's. And when the feechie opened his mouth to speak, the word he spoke sounded at first like a cry for mercy: "Hhhhhelp!" It was a cruel trick. Hyko's breath amounted, really, to an unfair advantage. The long, breathy "Hhhhhelp!" was like the opening of a furnace in Aidan's face, except that it wasn't just heat that blasted forth, but the nose-stinging, eye-burning vapor of old fish and wild onion that was the defining characteristic of feechie breath. Aidan reeled backward in horror, clutching his mouth and nose, trying to get his wits about him.

Hyko wasted no time. He mounted a fallen log, leaped from it, and laid his staggering opponent low with a smart elbow to the back of the head. But as Aidan fell, he grabbed Hyko's ankle and by sheer strength spun the feechie to the ground beside him. He flopped onto Hyko and pinned his shoulders to the ground.

Though Orlo was supposed to be the referee of the match, he was so enthralled with the rough-and-tumble action that a couple of seconds passed before it dawned on him to start counting. And when he did start, he counted very, very slowly: "Ooooooooonnnnne. . . ." The truth was, Orlo wanted to see one of the wrestlers stick the other's head in a tortoise hole. To Orlo, that seemed like a wrestling match with real style. He didn't want to see the match end with a pin. That was boring, unimaginative. And he certainly didn't want to see the match end so soon. So he slowed the count even more: "Twoooooooooooooooo. . . ."

Meanwhile, Hyko broke free and scrambled to his feet. He bulled Aidan to the ground, and the two of them writhed and rolled on the ground like a pair of fighting snakes. Orlo and Pobo cheered the match. Reluctant to take sides, they shouted words of encouragement without specifying whom they were intended to encourage.

"You get him, boy!"

"Stuff him down a turtle hole!"

"I saw that!"

The wrestlers migrated dangerously close to the cooking fire, which was still burning. Hyko's flying leg scattered hot coals and burning sticks well beyond the banked sand that formed the boundary of the fire. But soon they flopped away from the fire. Hyko was getting the better of Aidan now and was having some success cramming the civilizer's head into a tortoise hole. By Pobo's rule, a head-cram was deemed complete—and the match over—when both of the losing wrestler's ears were completely in the hole and not visible above ground. Hyko's head-cramming task was complicated because the tortoise hole wasn't as big around as Aidan's head.

Aidan's ears, like his mouth and nose, were full of sand, so it was hard to understand the chant Orlo and Pobo had struck up while he was being stuffed into a small hole in the ground. But when Hyko suddenly let go of his hair, Aidan raised his head and saw a broad sweep of wire grass being consumed by an orange flame, just a few feet from the cooking fire. Now he understood what Orlo and Pobo had been chanting: "Fire! Fire! Fire!"

Chapter Thirteen

Backfire

Aidan scrambled to his feet and ran toward the licking flames. He stomped at the burning grass, smothering the fire in boot-sized patches. The feechies joined, too, stomping as best they could. But even feechies aren't tough enough to stomp out a wildfire with bare feet.

A steady breeze from the west fanned the fire and it grew, carrying flames from one tuft of wire grass to the next. Aidan fetched his extra tunic from his backpack and used it to smother flames, but it was too late for that. The fire had stretched itself into a long line marching eastward before the prevailing wind. A small holly tree had already caught fire and sent popping cinders out ahead of the fire line. Little troops of flames licked around the bases of the big pine trees, looking to burst into magnificent flame among the long straw of the overstory. But the old trees resisted, and the ground fires died at their feet.

The vanguard of the fire kept marching onward. Rabbits fled before it, as did pine voles, little ground sparrows, and other animals that depended on the high, thick grass for cover. Rat snakes and cotton mice, normally predators and prey, entered a truce born of emergency and sought refuge together in the dark coolness of the tortoise burrows, deep below the crackling fire.

Behind the fire line a swath of charred and smoking ground expanded. But the fire was insatiable. It pushed eastward, devouring every blade of grass, every bush, every little sapling in its path. Aidan looked past the fire to the forest beyond. Dry wire grass waved as far as he could see—leagues and leagues of fuel for a fire that looked as if it might never stop.

The feechies were running in every direction, yelling and waving their arms but not doing anything helpful. They soon lost what little self-control they had and began crying and moaning, heartbroken at the prospect of their beautiful forest going up in flame. Hyko took it especially hard; his leg, after all, had kicked the burning log into the grass to set this conflagration in motion.

But they all snapped to attention when Aidan announced, "I know what to do."

Hyko wiped his eyes and sniffed a long, wet sniffle. "You do?"

They didn't understand what Aidan was doing when he pulled burning limbs out of the fire and handed one to each of them. But they were encouraged by the apparent sense of purpose with which he shouldered his pack and raised his own firebrand like a cavalry officer's sword. "Follow me!" he ordered, and as he ran across the smoking ground toward the fire line, the three feechies followed.

"Ow! Ow! Ooooh! Ow!"

"Hooo! Hooo! Hot! Hot!"

The poor feechies didn't have the benefit of a layer of boot leather between their feet and the hot ground, and the closer they came to the fire, the hotter it was.

"I'm 'bout to burn up!" complained Hyko above the crackle of flames. But neither he nor the other two feechies turned back.

"It's cooler on the other side!" shouted Aidan. And with that, he leaped into the chest-high hedge of flame. The feechies closed their eyes and followed him.

"Haa-wee!" Aidan shouted exultantly when he made it through the flames. He turned around just in time to see Hyko throw down his firebrand and barrel into him. Civilizer and feechie fell to the ground.

"Stop it!" yelled Aidan. "Stop it!" But Hyko didn't stop. He rolled Aidan over on his back as if to pin him. *These feechies don't know when to stop!* thought Aidan as he struggled to get away. Then Orlo and Pobo jumped into the fracas and started slapping at him.

"What's the matter with you!" Aidan screamed. He was good and angry now. A brushfire was bearing down on them, but all these feechies wanted to do was fight and wrestle.

"You're on fire!" shouted Hyko, and Aidan realized it was true. The flapping tail of his tunic had caught fire as he passed through the flames. The three feechies rolled him back and forth and slapped at his smoking tunic until they were sure the fire was out.

But there was little time to reflect on the near disaster. Aidan relit his smoldering firebrand in the encroaching fire line and led the feechies onward, ahead of the fire, across the open forest. He didn't stop until he was more than three long stone's throws away from the fire line. He stopped in a spot where the grass was sparser and more sand showed between the clumps.

The feechies' eyes grew wide when Aidan touched his firebrand to the wire grass and set it ablaze.

"What's a matter with you!" barked Orlo, stomping at the burning grass. "I thought we was going to fight this fire, not feed it!"

"It's called fighting fire with fire," Aidan explained. He touched off another clump of grass. "A wildfire can't burn what's already burned." He lit another tussock near his feet. "If we can make a backfire we can control, we might be able to kill the wild one."

Hyko was starting to understand. "We burn out the grass from this end, and when the wildfire gets here, it's got nowhere to go."

"As long as this one doesn't get away from us too," cautioned Aidan.

Hyko jigged around excitedly. Like all feechies, he liked playing with fire and was glad to have a good excuse. "Hee-haw! This civilizer's got what it takes!" He set his torch to a tussock of grass, then another and another.

"Whoa, horse!" laughed Aidan, stomping out one of Hyko's fires. "Don't make more fire than you can handle!"

Orlo and Pobo were skeptical of Aidan's scheme, but in the absence of a better plan, they touched their firebrands to the grass.

The westerly breeze tried to push the backfire into the firefighters. Occasional gusts sent them scrambling, stomping out fresh blazes. Aidan stomped and leaped like a buck-dancer and made good use of the long, broad rattlesnake hide as a fire beater to smother the flames. Since his feet were protected by boots, Aidan took sole responsibility for killing errant sparks while Orlo, Pobo, and Hyko broadened the reach of the backfire. Back and forth he ran, up and down, responding to the urgent cries of his men when a stray clump of grass ignited or a popping cinder threatened to set a bush ablaze.

The occasional gust of wind was a crisis, threatening to send the backfire in the wrong direction, to make it an accomplice in the ravages of the wildfire. And as the feechie crew succeeded in stretching out its line of defense, Aidan had farther to run and more emergencies to deal with.

They seemed to be making progress. A band of blackened wire grass grew longer and broader, and though it was ugly, it represented the best hope that the grass for miles beyond would be spared the same fiery fate. The wildfire lengthened its reach even as it was getting closer. The backfire still wasn't nearly long enough to contain it.

The strain of the work was starting to show on all the firefighters. The heat and smoke were exhausting. They were all blackened beyond recognition. And Aidan had been running in the smoke for close to an hour without a rest. He was getting discouraged, ready to surrender and let the wildfire burn to its heart's content, when an unfamiliar voice sounded behind them.

"What's going on here? Why you burning up my woods?"

The firefighters turned to see a hunting party of five feechies who had materialized from the forest. "Tombro!" Hyko shouted joyously to the strange feechie who had spoken. Tombro squinted, unable to recognize Hyko for the coating of soot and ash. "It's me, Hyko Vinesturgeon."

Tombro nodded his head slowly. "Yeah, I reckon you're Hyko. But with that black face, you look more like a old hog bear." He turned to the other two soot-blackened feechies. "Then you must be Orlo and Pobo?" He looked quizzically at Aidan, who was still running furiously up and down the line of the backfire and stomping at flames. Aidan was so thoroughly blackened that the newcomers didn't even notice he was a civilizer.

"That's Pantherbane," explained Orlo. "The civilizer."

The new feechies gaped in wonder. "*The* Pantherbane?" asked one of them.

"That's right," said Pobo. "Sure as you're standing there."

The hunters waved shyly at Aidan, who waved back, though he didn't stop his frantic dance to do so. "We need help," he announced. "A lot of help. We're making a backfire." He looked at the approaching wall of flame. It was only fifty strides away.

"Sure, sure," nodded Tombro eagerly, and his four companions nodded with him. None of them understood what Aidan was talking about, but they were honored to help the famous Pantherbane any way they could. Pobo fetched firebrands for them. Aidan pointed to the wildcat hide that one of the new feechies wore for a cape. "Can you use that for a fire beater?" he asked.

The feechie hesitated a moment. The cape was his most prized possession. Tombro had little patience with such foolishness. "Jerdo, give me that cat hide," he grumbled, unhooking the claw catch from around Jerdo's neck. "If Pantherbane needs help, we gonna help him."

The extra hands were a huge help to the firefighters who needed all the help they could get. The wind had picked up, and the wildfire was coming faster. Seven feechies were lighting fires now, and Aidan and Tombro worked frantically up and down the line, beating and stomping out fires that sprouted up ever more quickly.

When the leading edge of the wildfire was a mere ten strides from them, Aidan called a retreat. He wasn't sure what would happen when the two fires collided, and he didn't want anyone to get hurt.

The wildfire roared over the smaller backfire like a tidal wave. It looked unstoppable, throwing sparks and cinders in front, little flaming outriders scouting out new grass to burn, new bushes to swallow up. The fire made its own wind, searing waves that pulsed at the nine firefighters, who winced not just at the heat, but at the dread of the wildfire jumping their hard-won firebreak and swallowing the vast expanse of forest behind them.

A few flying sparks and airborne cinders did clear the firebreak and land in the flammable grass beyond. But vigilant firefighters quickly squelched them before the fire could find purchase. Most of the sparks, however, landed in the blackened trail of the backfire, where they died for lack of fuel. The main body of the wildfire spent itself. It had nowhere else to go, no way to propel itself farther.

At the south end of the line, however, the wildfire outflanked the backfire. For a few tense minutes it appeared enough flames had survived to grow again into an unmanageable blaze. But Tombro dropped to the ground and started digging furiously with a flat stone, about the size of his hand, that he pulled from his side pouch. The other seven feechies had similar tools in their own pouches, and together they were able to dig just enough of a trench to slow the fire.

The fire jumped the feechies' trench but not all at once. As the flames licked across, the firefighters were ready for them and snuffed them out. Aidan handed his snakeskin to Pobo and took off his own tunic to use as a fire beater. Jerdo's cat hide was a blackened mess by now, but the three fire beaters were more than enough to contain the last remnants of the fire.

"Hee-haw!" yodeled Tombro. "We whupped it!"

Aidan surveyed the black and smoking scene before him. "We whupped it," he rasped, almost too blistered and exhausted and thirsty to care. "We whupped it."

Chapter Fourteen

Seep Hole

Aidan squeezed cool mud between his fingers and dug his blistered feet in the mud beneath the shallow water to soothe them. A huge mud-coated sycamore leaf was plastered on his scorched brow like a cooling rag. Tombro had led the troop of firefighters to this shady seep hole to recover from the rigors of their day. Three of Tombro's hunting party stayed at the fire site to make sure the smoldering fire didn't burst again into flame. But everybody else—Aidan, Hyko, Orlo, Pobo, Tombro, and Jerdo—was sprawled in the ankle-deep water of the seep hole, lolling in the mud.

"This is living," observed Pobo, glopping a handful of sticky mud onto his chest and slathering it around.

"A leech!" squealed Orlo, raising his leg out of the muddy water. Aidan blanched at the sight of a glistening black sluglike mass, about the size of a pinky finger, attached to the feechie's ankle. And he felt sick when Orlo pried it loose and popped it whole into his mouth.

"Mmmmm," Orlo murmured contentedly as he chewed. "Could things get any better?"

"Lucky," muttered Hyko as he checked his own arms and legs for leeches.

Aidan was starting to doze, but he was awakened by a question from Tombro. "Hey, Pantherbane," he called. "What'd you say your civilizer name was?"

"It's Aidan, Aidan Errolson."

"Errolson?" asked Tombro. "What's that name supposed to mean?"

"Well," Aidan began, not sure what the feechie was asking, "it means I'm the son of Errol. That's how all civilizer last names work. I'm Aidan son of Errol so my name's Aidan Errolson. My father's the son of Finlay, so his name is Errol Finlayson."

"So civilizer names don't mean much of anything then," observed Tombro. "Every feechie name tells a story—tells about something you done or something one of your people done." He was up on one elbow now, the better to gesture while he talked. "Take my name," he said, "Tombro Timberbeaver. My daddy won the swampwide log-cutting contest five years straight and never picked up a ax." Aidan looked doubtful, but Tombro pressed on. "He had a family of beavers he trained. And when he told them beavers where to gnaw, they whirled in there and fairly made the chips fly! That's how my people came to be called Timberbeavers."

Aidan smiled wanly. He wasn't sure he believed Tombro's story, but he didn't want to offend by expressing doubt. He had already survived one feechie fight that day and didn't feel up for another.

"Ask Hyko," suggested Tombro. "Ask Hyko where his last name come from."

"All right," Aidan obliged. "Hyko, how'd you get your last name?"

Hyko smiled. It was a favorite feechie pastime to tell name stories, and the story of the Vinesturgeons, Hyko's clan, was always a favorite. "My granddaddy used to hunt sturgeon when they come upriver," he began. "Had him a little flatboat, and he'd stand up in the bow like this here." He got to his feet and stood in a crouch, feet apart. He raised his right fist to his ear as if he had a spear at the ready. "Them big, ugly fish'd come cruising up the river—some of them bigger than Granddaddy's boat—and when he saw a big fin break the water . . ." He reared back and flung his imaginary spear at Jerdo, who happened to be lazing directly in front of him.

"That's when the fun would commence. 'Cause the spear had a long vine attached to it, and Granddaddy hung on to that vine for a owdacious ride. Up the river. Down the river. Across the river." Hyko zigzagged around the seep hole, pretending to be towed this way and that. "He'd hang on, and that ugly old sturgeon would pull the boat ever which way until he just played out.

"But Granddaddy was a little feller, and sometimes the big fish'd pull the vine right out his hands. He lost two fish in one morning that way—two good spears too. He told his fishing buddies he didn't aim to miss the next one.

"Sure enough, he speared him a third sturgeon that morning. And this'n didn't pull the vine outta Granddaddy's hands. It pulled him clean outta the boat, but Granddaddy wouldn't turn loose. It dragged him underwater. Granddaddy still wouldn't turn loose. Ever now and then his head popped out of the water, first here, then there, now way over yonder." He pointed another zigzag. "But still he wouldn't turn loose.

"The sturgeon finally played out, and Granddaddy's buddies fished Granddaddy and the fish both outta the river. They hung Granddaddy upside down from a tree limb just to drain all the water out him. But they figured out why he didn't let go of that vine: He'd done tied it 'round his waist! He couldn't have let go if he'd a wanted to." Aidan and the feechies hooted with laughter. "And from that day to this," concluded Hyko, "all my people been called Vinesturgeon."

Aidan applauded Hyko's performance. He was fascinated by the feechies' naming customs. "So Dobro Turtlebane," he asked, "where does his name come from?"

"Oh, the Turtlebanes are a clan of fierce turtle hunters," answered Hyko, "the bane of turtles' existence."

"How about your cousin, Theto Elbogator?"

Hyko was ready with that story too. "There's a crook of the Tam the feechiefolks calls the Elbow. Used to be a big alligator lived there. We called him the Elbow gator. He'd smash up boats that floated through, eat whatever folks fell out. Theto kilt that alligator. Ate him too. Ever since, his family's been called the Elbogators. Before that, they was just plain old Sands, like Orlo and Pobo there."

Aidan was confused. "I thought you weren't related!" he said, looking at Orlo and Pobo.

"We ain't," answered Pobo. "Sands is just the name you get stuck with if you or none of your folks ain't done nothing special."

"If you ain't kilt no ravaging critters or won no contests or half-drownded yourself chasing after a fish, folks just call you Sands," Orlo explained.

"We're just as common and no'count as dirt, I reckon," moaned Pobo. "So folks calls us Sands." Orlo and Pobo both looked to be on the point of tears, and the other feechies were quick to offer words of assurance.

"You'll get you a name one of these days."

"You boy's ain't all that no'count."

Hyko thought about giving Pobo a hug, but Pobo drew back as if to punch him in the nose. Hyko changed his mind, thinking it better to change the subject instead. "Pantherbane," he called, "how come you're out here nearbout to Feechiefen, instead of across the river where civilizers belong?"

Aidan decided to tell the whole truth on that score for the first time since he left Tambluff. "I'm going into the swamp to fetch a frog orchid for King Darrow."

"You?" asked Jerdo, a little sarcastically. "Headed into Feechiefen alone?" The feechies all laughed at the idea of a civilizer—even Pantherbane himself—venturing into the Feechiefen alone.

Aidan ignored their mocking laughter. "I was hoping I could find a feechie guide. Do any of you know where the frog orchid grows?"

The feechies just shrugged. "I don't know 'bout no frog orchid," said Hyko. "The Feechiefen is full of orchids—pink orchids, white orchids, yellow orchids, purple."

"Some of them bigger around than your head," offered Orlo. "Some of them would set on your fingernail."

"There's orchids that grows on the ground, orchids that grows on trees," said Tombro.

"Some orchids grows on other orchids," Hyko continued. "I've seen orchids shaped like a turtle, orchids shaped like a gator's mouth. There's some that smells like rotten lizard eggs. But the one you call a frog orchid, I don't know what that is."

Aidan's face fell. He had assumed that any feechie he met in the swamp would be able to take him straight to the frog orchid. "So you've never heard the Frog Orchid Chant?" The feechies all shook their heads. Aidan recited a couple of lines to see if it jogged anyone's memory: "In deepest swamp, in house of bears, / An orchid in the spring appears."

"House of bears?" snorted Jerdo. "That don't narrow things down too much. Ever dry spot in the swamp's a house for bears."

"Unless it's talking about Bearhouse Island," suggested Orlo.

"Well, I ain't guiding nobody to Bearhouse!" yawped Pobo.

There was a general grumble of agreement.

"Me neither!"

"I heard that!"

"Uh-uh, not me."

"I'm skeered of Bearhouse Island," confessed Hyko, "and I'm fearless."

"Where's Bearhouse?" asked Aidan.

"Spang in the middle of the swamp," Hyko said. "Five days' poling from the swamp edge."

"That's five days for a feechie, born and raised in the Feechiefen," put in Orlo. "And that don't count the time you'd spend fighting off the biggest alligators in the swamp."

"But even that ain't the worst part of it," continued Jerdo. "The worst part's the feechiefolks that runs things on Bearhouse."

"Chief Larbo's band," Hyko explained. "And them boys is mean."

"Aren't all feechies mean?" Aidan asked.

"Well, sure," said Pobo, with a hint of pride in his voice, "but we ain't talking about regular feechie mean. Folks that's too nasty to live with the rest of us, that's who joins up with Larbo's band."

"Folks what don't care a lizard's tail for the Feechie Code," said Orlo.

"Folks what don't love their mamas." Tombro shivered as he said it.

The feechies' description of Larbo's band of outlaws made Aidan think of the attacks on Last Camp. "Somebody's been attacking a hunting camp on the other side of the river," he said. "I think it's feechies. Could it be Larbo's band?"

"On the civilizer side?" Tombro shook his head. "Even Larbo wouldn't attack on the civilizer side."

"But they shot from the treetops," said Aidan. "And when they ran away, they ran away through the treetops. Civilizers can't do that."

Hyko's brow wrinkled. "That do sound like feechiefolks . . ."

"You say they was shooting," said Tombro. "What kind of arrows did they shoot?"

"I saved one," said Aidan. He pulled the white-feathered arrow out of his quiver and handed it to Tombro.

"See there?" said Tombro triumphantly. "Cold-shiny arrowhead. Can't be feechie."

"But that shaft . . ." Hyko began.

"What about it?" Tombro retorted.

"It's black bamboo. Feechiefen's the only place where black bamboo grows. A civilizer couldn'ta made this arrow."

Taking the arrow from Tombro, Orlo fingered the white feathers. "Egret feathers," he observed. "Few days ago, me and Pobo come up on a egret rookery where somebody'd kilt all the birds and left them dead on the ground—just plucked out the big plume feathers and left them there."

"Pitifullest thing I ever seen," said Pobo.

"Plume hunters are shooting out the rookeries on the civilizer side too," said Aidan.

The feechies grew quiet, trying to figure out what it meant. Hyko was the first to speak. "I don't know what's going on exactly," he admitted, "but I do know that there's feechies breaking the code, and that brings trouble on every feechie in the swamp."

"Cold-shiny arrowheads . . ." Pobo's lip curled in disgust. "Next thing, folks'll be building civilizer houses all over the swamp and riding around on smelly horses and covering ever dry spot with furball, civilizer sheep. What kind of feechie would shoot a cold-shiny arrowhead?"

"Maybe the same kind of feechie what shoots out a whole egret rookery," answered Orlo.

"And attacking civilizers on their side of the river . . ." Hyko shook his head. "That'll just bring the civilizers to Feechiefen, with their horses and their cold-shiny spears."

"I wish they'd try," boasted Jerdo, puffing out his chest. "Can't no civilizers whup us in our own swamp!"

"'Course not," answered Hyko, "but we still don't want a bunch of civilizers tromping around in the Feechiefen." He rubbed his head nervously. "We got to hold a swamp council. We got to do something 'bout this before it's too late."

Chapter Fifteen

Into the Feechiefen

The swamp council was set to convene three nights later at Scoggin Mound, a tiny island one day's journey into the swamp's interior. Leaving before sunrise the day after the brushfire, the feechies dispersed across the northern part of the swamp to recruit feechies from various bands to participate in the council.

Aidan traveled with Tombro. Scoggin Mound was Tombro's home village, and it was his responsibility to get things in order for the council. He and Aidan were to go directly to Scoggin Mound, or as directly as the Feechiefen would let them.

They continued due south through the pine flats. Then, around noon, Aidan noticed the vegetation abruptly changed. The open forest of big pines and wire grass was replaced by the enveloping greenness of lowland swamp. The ground grew soft beneath their feet and mucky more than sandy. Vines and thickets slowed their progress, and ferocious bugs descended from all sides.

Aidan tried to take the insect bites in stride, but the stinging flies were worse than anything he had ever encountered in the land of the civilizers. He slapped, swatted, and waved his arms, but they kept coming. He could hardly pay attention to where he was going, and twice he fell, tripped by vines that snaked across the ground.

The tanglewood closed in tighter as they pushed southward, and it soon became apparent that Aidan's backpack couldn't make the trip. Every low-hanging branch seemed to catch it and snatch Aidan backward, as if the forest itself were reaching out to hinder the civilizer's progress toward its most secret places.

When Tombro finished disentangling Aidan from a grapevine for the third time, he said, "That's enough of that, Pantherbane. Either you leave that civilizer backpouch, or I'm leaving you." Aidan knew Tombro was right. But he still couldn't bear the thought of leaving behind everything he had so carefully packed for his quest.

"Whatever you got in there," assured Tombro, "it ain't what you need. You headed into the Feechiefen Swamp. Civilizer ways won't be much good to you. Only feechie ways." He casually waved away an attacking deerfly. "And the grace of the One God."

In spite of himself, Tombro did have a look through Aidan's belongings, just to see if a few things might be of use. He opened Aidan's water bladder and took a sip of the clear, pure water, fresh from the spring at Last Camp. He spewed it out and staggered around as if he had been poisoned.

"Aaaach!" he choked, twisting his face into a grimace of disgust. "How can you drink that stuff?" He threw the water bladder over his shoulder. "Ain't no need to haul that nasty stuff all the way to Scoggin Mound. Feechiefen's full of water, nice black water. And there's always a surprise floating in it, for extra flavor."

He found Aidan's quill pen and palmetto paper in the backpack. He took a bite out of the paper, but chew as he might, he couldn't get it to go down. "That stuff ain't fit to eat," he declared as he balled it up and threw it into the bushes. He held up Aidan's pen and laughed. "You can get plenty of feathers in the Feechiefen. And a heap prettier than that'un. Ain't no reason to bring one from over the river."

He uncorked Aidan's inkpot and was about to take a swig when Aidan snatched it away from him and threw it into the woods to save Tombro the trouble. Tombro tried to throw away Aidan's hunting knife, on the grounds that it was made of cold-shiny. But Aidan insisted on keeping it. The feechie relented but only after making Aidan promise to get a proper stone knife at the first opportunity. He did, however, convince Aidan to leave behind his bow and steel-tipped arrows, promising to get him a smaller feechie bow and arrows the minute they arrived at Scoggin Mound.

Tombro laughed at Aidan's rope, pointing out that every tree was festooned with vines of every size that would do just as well. Everything else in Aidan's pack met with similar ridicule, except the alligator jerky. That was something Tombro could see the use of.

Tombro was also pleased to find the rattlesnake hide that Aidan had used for a fire beater the previous day. "Hold on, now," he said excitedly as he unrolled the skin.

The smoke and heat from the fire had crudely tanned it. Tombro rubbed the scaly hide between his palms, then snapped it taut, testing its strength. He held it up to Aidan's waist. It was more than long enough to wrap around; it almost went around twice. And it was broad enough to cover halfway to his knees. "You got yourself a kilt," he whooped, "just like a natural-born he-feechie. You don't need that civilizer getup at all! You can dress like one of us."

Aidan saw the benefit in going native. Feechiefen was one place where it was best to blend in with the locals as much as possible. There was no need to draw attention to the fact he was a civilizer. Tombro went in search of just the right gray mud with which to coat Aidan, both for bug protection and camouflage.

Meanwhile, Aidan took off his civilizer clothes and wrapped the snakeskin around his waist. It was crinkly and stiff, but it was comfortable enough, and in the sticky heat of the wetlands, it would be cooler than his civilizer clothes. Believing he struck a dashing figure as a he-feechie, Aidan felt an unavoidable twinge of pride. But he was eager for Tombro to return with the mud. The mosquitoes and biting flies were making a banquet of his bare chest and back.

When Tombro came back with two big handfuls of foul-smelling gray mud, he hooted at the sight of the big white civilizer standing in his civilizer boots, holding his kilt up with one hand and furiously slapping at bugs with the other. But he applied the mud as quickly as he could. In spite of its smell, the mud soothed Aidan's existing bug bites and protected him from getting new ones. In his side pouch, Tombro had an extra kilt clasp, made from the fangs of a rattlesnake. He fastened Aidan's kilt with it, freeing the civilizer's second hand.

Tombro took a step back to look at his handiwork. "Not too bad," he mused. "You're the right colors, at least, and you smell a little more like a feechie." He looked at Aidan's close-cropped hair. "Your hair needs some help. But you can't grow a mane like this in a day." Tombro ran his muddy fingers along the matted hair that draped down his neck. "Maybe we can skin out a muskrat. You could wear its pelt for a wig," he suggested. "When we get to Scoggin Mound, you can borrow one of my turtle helmets."

Tombro tried to convince Aidan to remove his boots. "Ain't nobody going to mistake you for a feechie with them stump-clompers on your feet," he said. But Aidan pointed out that civilizer feet were much more tender than feechie feet and that his feet couldn't survive the rigors of the swamp without the protection of boots. Tombro gave in, but not without wondering aloud how civilizers managed to survive in a place like Corenwald if they weren't any tougher than that.

With Aidan's load thus lightened and the vegetation growing thicker, it wasn't long before he and Tombro took to the treetops. Onward they went, limb to limb toward the heart of the Feechiefen. The understory was so thick that Aidan rarely saw the forest floor. And when he did see all the way to the bottom of the trees, he saw water as often as he saw dry land. On and on it went.

After an hour or so of tree walking, they took a short rest in the top of a big sweet gum tree. "Big swamp," Aidan remarked. "But the Feechiefen's not so different from some of the swamps around Longleaf, where I'm from."

Tombro gave Aidan a quizzical look. "Feechiefen? This ain't Feechiefen. This is the little scrub swamp that borders it. When we get to Feechiefen, you gonna know it."

Two hours later, the dense scrub opened into the Feechiefen. And, as Tombro had promised, there was no mistaking it. It was a place of terrible beauty, forbidding and at the same time mesmerizing. Enormous cypress trees—taller even than longleaf pines—soared into the sky from flanged bases so broad that Aidan could imagine flatboats full of standing feechies completely hidden behind each one.

The still water was as black as night itself, and yet no mirror could reflect the sky and clouds more perfectly. The surface of the water was another world, an upside-down world. The effect was dizzying. The same cypress trees that speared upward into the sky also plunged downward to an identical sky below. The white-bellied cranes that glided above glided upside down in the lower sky. A heron stood knee-deep in the water, joined at the knee with its upside-down twin, which bobbed its long beak upward to the water's surface as the upright bird bobbed down.

Aidan had often daydreamed about the Feechiefen. But he hadn't imagined this. He had pictured the

Feechiefen as a bigger version of the swamps and tangle-wood forests he knew so well. But this was another thing altogether. The swamps Aidan knew were borderlands, places of transition between river and dry land. He could see now there was nothing transitional about this place. The Feechiefen was its own place, as self-contained as an inland sea.

There were rivers in the Feechiefen, as Aidan would soon learn. But there were no riverbanks. The rivers that flowed through the vast swamp were bordered by more water, not by dry land. There was dry land in Feechiefen too. But except for a few real islands, most of the land was just floating mats of moss burped up from the bottom of the swamp. A few plants took root and flourished—plants whose seeds blew in, floated in, or rode in on the feet of birds. Sometimes the floating islands joined together to form quite large plots of land. But any sense of permanence on those floating islands was only an illusion. They might sink back into the black water any day.

"Feechiefen," Tombro whispered reverently at their first sight of the great swamp. Aidan saw a tear form in the feechie's eye. He could see why this son of the swamp would be so homesick.

"How long have you been away?" Aidan asked.

"Four days," answered Tombro. "Four long days."

Aidan followed Tombro through a few more treetops along the edge of the swamp. "There's one," Tombro declared, and the two of them scampered to the base of a tree where a little flat-bottomed boat was pulled up into the bushes. A boat pole was there, too, and in quick order

Tombro had situated Aidan in the front of the boat and slid it into the water. Tombro stood in the stern, and with quick, nimble strokes he poled toward open water.

"Is this your boat?" asked Aidan.

"That's one way to say it, I reckon," the feechie answered.

"You didn't steal it, did you?"

"Can't steal a boat," said Tombro, exasperated once again by the civilizer's peculiar notions. "Boats don't belong to nobody. So how could you steal one?" The feechies, Tombro explained, had an ingenious method for handling the ownership of boats. On his tenth birthday, and every tenth birthday after that, every feechie was required to build a flatboat and give it to the chieftain of his band. The chieftain, in turn, gave all boats to the Feechiefen. So then, any feechie who needed to make a crossing was welcome to any boat he could find. After crossing, he left the boat where it landed, and any feechie who came along later was welcome to use it. The boat Tombro was plying across the water, therefore, wasn't his exactly, but it wasn't anybody else's either.

The boat slid as smoothly and soundlessly as a water spider across the still water. Behind, Tombro's push pole stirred up a little cloud of bottom litter in the shallow water. But ahead, the water was a sheet of black glass. Tombro nosed the craft between the funnels of the cypress trees, turning right and left, confidently navigating by a method Aidan didn't understand.

Feechiefen wasn't a tangled mess like the floodplain swamps around Longleaf. The cypress trees and gum trees grew close together, as closely as the trees in the densest forests. But the forest floor was black water, not the rich soil of the floodplain. So the vines that often choked the forest were uncommon in the Feechiefen, except on the islands. Instead, the trees were draped with air plants that need no soil to grow—graybeard moss that swayed in great dangling masses, tree ferns shaped like hanging deer antlers, and orchids of seemingly infinite variety, the most splendid flowers Aidan had ever seen. But he never saw one that looked like a flying frog.

And the alligators! On every side, their eyes and rounded nostrils knobbed out of the water, and their broad, ridged backs looked like little islands in the swamp, ever-shifting, appearing and disappearing as the boat traversed their territory.

In time, Tombro guided the little boat to an opening in the cypress trees, and Aidan could make out a narrow channel of slow-moving water where trees didn't grow. Tombro put the boat in the channel and headed down its stream. It was easier poling here, with no trees to steer around and a current, however slow, to help them along. Tombro felt exuberant, and he belted out a yodeling swamp holler:

Hoo lee ooo lee,
Hoo lee ooo lee,
Pappy's coming home.
Hoo lee ooo lee,
Hoo lee ooo lee,
Put my supper on!

In the west, a blazing orange sun descended to meet its twin sun in the surface of the water. In the east, the high-piled clouds reflected the rays of the setting sun in fantastic gold-trimmed pinks and purples.

As dusk approached, however, the stillness was shattered by the beginnings of the swamp's night song. The frogs in their thousands—tens of thousands—set up their spring holler, a pleasing cacophony of a hundred different pitches and timbres. The alligators, too, began their bellowing and boasting, which echoed across the swamp like thunder. The big bull alligators wagged their massive heads in mutual threat. Swamp water cascaded from their open jaws, and to Aidan it appeared that steam was billowing from their nostrils. Their lashing tails whipped the black water to froth.

Tombro seemed unconcerned, even though any one of those crashing tails could smash their boat to splinters. He glanced up at a flock of wood storks sailing overhead toward their rookery. "Baldheads coming to roost," he remarked. "I reckon we ought to too."

Tombro poled alongside a little island of floating moss, about six or eight strides across. "See won't that little blow-up hold you," he suggested. Aidan was alarmed by Tombro's obvious doubt that the floating island could support his weight. He pictured himself sinking into the swamp's dark waters and, before he could clamber back into the boat, being shredded by alligators fighting for his carcass. But he was eager to show that he had the gumption to make it in the Feechiefen, so he stood in the bow of the boat and began to step off onto the island.

"Ipp! Ipp!" warned Tombro. "Hands and knees! Hands and knees! Don't punch through on the first step."

Aidan crouched and reached one hand toward the moss. The island rocked crazily, sending out waves in circles that nearly tipped the boat. Aidan looked back doubtfully at Tombro, but Tombro waved him forward. "Get along," he said. "Slow won't work. Got to skitter up there like a muskrat."

Aidan skittered, trying to think like a muskrat, not like a civilizer in the middle of the Feechiefen Swamp— not like a civilizer in danger of sinking to its murky bottom at any moment. The flexible ground beneath his hands and knees rolled and bucked as if it were trying to sling Aidan into the water. But it didn't sink. Aidan crawled a step, then another, watching for any sign of water seeping through the ground beneath his fingers.

His progress was halted, however, by a hissing sound that he knew very well. When he looked up, his face was two feet away from the gaping pink mouth of an alligator. His first thought was to beat a hasty retreat, but the ground was too shaky for any quick movements. He couldn't run. He couldn't fight. The alligator gave another terrifying hiss and moved another slow step toward him. From where he crouched, head-on to the alligator, Aidan could see only mouth—big, pink tongue, widespread jaws, and two arcs of gleaming white teeth.

Behind him, Aidan heard Tombro chuckling. The end of Tombro's push pole slid along the surface of the moss, past Aidan, to jab at the alligator. The powerful jaws snapped on the pole end, and then Aidan realized what Tombro was laughing at. The alligator, now that Aidan could see past its mouth, was only a small one, no more than four feet long.

"Scurry off, little gator," Tombro wheedled. He poked again at the alligator. "Us big gators want your spot." The alligator left the little island, though it did offer a few bad-natured hisses as it slid off the back edge.

Tombro crawled gingerly onto the island. It held both civilizer and feechie without sinking. It was almost dark by now, and before long Aidan and Tombro were on their backs waiting for sleep to come, awed by the brilliant stars of a Feechiefen night. Below the Hunter's Belt, Aidan imagined he saw a new constellation: the Frog Orchid. Surely he was getting closer to it. Yes, the Feechiefen was daunting, but he had good and capable feechies at his side. Perhaps it wouldn't be long before he could return triumphantly to Tambluff Castle—frog orchid in hand, a hard-won gift for a king who would never again have reason to doubt his loyalty.

Beside him, Tombro chuckled. "When you see them big jaws head-on, every gator looks big enough to swaller you whole, don't he?"

"Yes," answered Aidan, "he sure does."

Chapter Sixteen

Scoggin Mound

t was an hour past noon the next day when Tombro poled the flatboat to the landing at Scoggin Mound. It was a bustling village. Actually, it was more of a base camp than a village. Most of the feechies who lived there—even the wee-feechies—spent more time elsewhere than they did at Scoggin Mound. Still, it was a more permanent settlement than Aidan would have thought possible for feechiefolk. Huts with palm-thatched roofs dotted the little island, and a few feechies walked back and forth balancing clay pots full of water, berries, or fish caught from the surrounding swamp.

The first people to notice Tombro and Aidan were a crowd of wee-feechies dressed in possum and muskrat hides and kicking a pine cone around a bare patch of sand a few strides from the landing.

"Tombro! Tombro!" they shouted.

"Did you bring me a turtle?"

"Did you bring any sugarcane?"

Then one of the wee-feechies noticed Aidan. "Ooook!" she shouted. "That's a big'un!"

"What happened to your hair, feller?" asked another wee-feechie. Aidan suddenly felt self-conscious of his bare neck. Even the wee-feechies wore their hair short in the front and long in the back.

"Craney-crow snapped it off, I reckon," theorized one of the wee-feechies.

"It never did," retorted one of the others. "You just skeered of craney-crows, Hendo. That's the only reason you'd say such a turtle-brain thing."

Hendo tackled his tormentor without even bothering to complete the rudeswap, and the two wee-feechies rolled around on the sand for awhile. But the others paid them little mind. They were more interested in the peculiar he-feechie Tombro had brought to their island. One of them elbowed his nearest neighbor and pointed at Aidan's boots. "What happened to your feets, feller?"

"Ooook!" gasped another. "His toes is gone!"

A bold wee-feechie with golden curls and a muskrat dress marched over to Aidan and stomped on the top of his boot. She barely came up to his knees.

"Margu!" scolded Tombro. "You ain't treating our visitor very friendly."

"I ain't trying to be friendly," she snarled. "I don't like him."

"Me neither," called one of the others.

"I don't like him a bit."

With that, all of the wee-feechies fell on Aidan, stomping his toes and kicking his boots. One of them bit his knee. Tombro shooed at them as if they were a pack of yippy dogs. "Scoot," he commanded. "Clear out, you owdacious scapers!"

"I want to know why he's so funny looking," demanded one of the wee-feechies.

"Yeah, Tombro. How come this feller's so ugly?"

"'Cause he can't help it," answered Tombro over the offended chatter of the wee-feechies. "'Cause he's a civilizer."

The little mob fell back a step, flabbergasted.

"But he's a good civilizer," Tombro quickly added, afraid the little ones would regroup for a second, more ferocious attack. "This here's Pantherbane." The wee-feechies looked dubious. "You know about Pantherbane, don't you?"

"My mama says there ain't no good civilizers."

"My mama says civilizers don't like nothing but cutting down trees."

"My daddy says they like sheep and horses better than they like the wild critters what belong on this island."

Though Aidan had defeated a panther, five plume hunters, and even a seven-foot Pyrthen, the wee-feechies of Scoggin Mound were too much for him. He didn't know how to answer their accusations against him. So he did something that, at the time, seemed an appropriately feechie thing to do. He hooked his fingers in his lips and pulled them wide to show all his teeth, crossed his eyes, stuck out his tongue, and roared like a bear. The wee-feechies scattered and ran screaming toward the middle of the island, their long hair streaming behind them.

"Civilizer!" one of then shrieked.

"He tried to eat me!"

"A civilizer's on the island!"

"He's going to civilize us all!"

Tombro and Aidan roared with laughter and followed the little ones toward the island's center where the village fire burned, the center of feechie life on Scoggin Mound.

They had just come into sight of the main hut circle when the *pffffffft* of a flying arrow burned through the air just inches from Aidan's left ear. In the middle distance, a white-haired she-feechie was notching a second arrow to her bow. Tombro threw Aidan on the ground and stood in front of him, blocking him from the old woman's arrow.

"Aunt Seku!" he yelled. "Don't shoot!"

"Move out the way, Tombro," she squawked. "That feller's tricked you. He ain't a feechie. He's a civilizer spy!" Her teeth were missing, and her collapsing gums made her chin jut out with an extra measure of determination.

"No, Aunt Seku," pleaded Tombro. "This is Pantherbane. He's a feechiefriend."

Aunt Seku kept her bowstring pulled taut and kept her left eye closed. She was drawing down on her target, waiting for Tombro to move just an inch to give her a shot. "If he's a feechiefriend, how come he's trying to eat my grandbabies?"

"Those young'uns was just skeered and addle-headed," called Tombro. "Pantherbane ain't gonna eat nobody. He's got the feechiemark, Aunt Seku. Come over here and look."

Seku lowered her bow and arrow and walked cautiously toward the civilizer. Aidan rose to his feet, and the old she-feechie grabbed him by the forearm to inspect it. "I don't see no feechiemark," she growled.

"Look again, Auntie," Tombro reassured her. "It's there."

Seku spat on Aidan's arm and rubbed the foamy glob with two wizened fingers. The gray mud dissolved away, and the feechiemark appeared—the curling alligator, red and fierce, Aidan's passport into the world of the feechies.

Seku's manner softened in an instant. "Bless your goozlum! Bless your innards! You *are* Pantherbane!" She hugged his neck and stood on her tiptoes to pat his head. "Such a fine-looking boy," she cooed. "For a civilizer."

Aunt Seku insisted that the travelers come to her hut for a snack before they saw another soul. "I found these grub worms this morning," she announced proudly as she placed a clay bowl between Aidan and Tombro. "They're still alive." Aidan could see that for himself. The grubs writhed in a white, tangled mass that made the civilizer's stomach turn. Tombro dug greedily into the bowl, but Aunt Seku slapped his hand with a switch she kept for such occasions. "Get your hand out them grubs till Pantherbane gets some, you owdacious villain!"

All eyes were on Aidan as he pulled a fat white grub from the top of the pile. He tried not to think about the stubby legs that grew from each of its bulging segments or about the black pinchers that served for its mouth. He thought it best just to swallow without chewing, to get it over faster. But on the way down, the grub grabbed Aidan's tonsil with its pinchers and held on for dear life. It refused to go down.

Aunt Seku watched eagerly for Aidan's pleased reaction. When his eyes watered from the pain of having a live grub attached to his tonsil, Seku mistook his tears for tears of joy. The grub went down at last, and to Aidan's relief and gratitude, Tombro took more than his share of the grubs. Aidan was able to make it through the rest of the interview with Aunt Seku without further incident.

"Sorry I was jubulous of you when you first come up, Pantherbane," said Seku. "It's just that I been seeing some peculiar things around here." She pushed the grub bowl toward Aidan, who patted his stomach to signal that he couldn't eat another bite. "The other day, little Berdo come in here telling about a man in the trees, wearing a shirt made outta cold-shiny circles. I figured it was just a wee-feechie tale. But then Hendo come into my hut yesterday with a cold-shiny arrowhead he found in the woods.

"When the young'uns set up such a calaberment today about a civilizer on Scoggin Mound, it made me feel a little tetchy." She pointed at Aidan's gleaming hunting knife. "I seen that shiny thing, and I figured the civilizers was here to get us sure."

"I'm sorry I scared you, Aunt Seku, and the wee-feechies too," said Aidan. "I'm just glad you fired a warning shot."

"That weren't a warning shot," answered Seku. "That was a shaky shot from an old she-feechie what's about wore out." She laughed a jolly, cackling laugh. "I was aiming to shoot you dead."

As he had promised, Tombro provided Aidan with a tortoiseshell helmet, a short feechie bow and stone-tipped arrows, and a stone knife. They couldn't do anything about Aidan's unfortunate haircut, and Tombro let him keep his civilizer boots. They left his cold-shiny knife with Aunt Seku for safekeeping.

Throughout the rest of the day, feechies from all over the northern end of the Feechiefen arrived at Scoggin Mound for the next night's swamp council. They came throughout the night, too, and all the next day. Most of them bore stories similar to the ones Aunt Seku had told. A dying deer, escaped from the hunter who shot it, was found to have been wounded with a steel-tipped arrow. A scout had seen what he believed to be the glint of cold-shiny armor in the treetops at Bug Neck. A hunter had heard the unfamiliar clank of metal in the bay forest of Long Strand.

Feechies from the bands that roamed the deepest interior of the swamp reported seeing a near-constant billow of smoke rising from Bearhouse Island—not the smoke of cooking fires but the thicker, blacker smoke of a more intense fire. And feechies from every band told stories of their meanest, most difficult bandmates switching over to Chief Larbo's band.

Throughout the day, Aidan kept hoping Dobro would show up. Feechies came by the dozen, but none of Chief Gergo's band appeared. The little island buzzed with talk of cold-shiny spears, cold-shiny knives, slaughtered plume birds, and falling trees on Bearhouse Island.

Aidan wondered what they would have left to talk about at that night's swamp council.

Fifty feechies or more came up to butt heads and introduce themselves to the great Pantherbane who, they had heard, had skinned a panther alive, eaten an alligator whole, and grabbled three catfish on one dive at Bayberry Creek. They all wanted to tell the great Pantherbane where they were and what they were doing the day the feechies and the civilizers together routed the Pyrthens in the Eechihoolee Forest. Fifty times Aidan explained how it was his quest for the frog orchid, and not a desire to fight Chief Larbo, that had brought him to the swamp. But no one seemed to know anything about the frog orchid.

With every introduction, every friendly head-butt, Aidan kept one eye out for Dobro. Then, around midafternoon, Dobro, Doyno, Branko, Odo, and Rabbo—the delegation from Chief Gergo's band—arrived at last from Bug Neck. "I heard old Pantherbane was here," Dobro whooped, slapping Aidan on the back. "Come to fetch him a flower!"

After a warm reunion with Aidan, Doyno, Branko, Odo, and Rabbo melted into the crowd to repeat their own stories about the day Pantherbane first fell in with Chief Gergo's band. Meanwhile, Dobro and Aidan sought out a quiet slough away from the hubbub of the settlement, where they would have privacy to catch up on events. Along the way, Aidan told how he came to be in the Feechiefen. He told of King Darrow's jealous rage and his sending Aidan on a quest for the frog orchid, the only cure for his melancholy.

Dobro shook his head at the underhanded, convoluted dealings of the civilizers. "That ain't the feechie way," he said. "If I want your nose busted, I ball up my fist and I bust it; then I take whatever might be coming to me. I don't tell you to walk into a tree and hope you bust it yourself."

"That makes for a lot of nose busting, doesn't it?" asked Aidan.

"Maybe so," answered Dobro. "But you bust a feller's nose, he busts yours, and the whole thing's over. Things don't boil and bubble till you decide you want to kill a feller instead of just busting his nose." He swished a stick in the water, watching the trail of tan bubbles swirl on the black surface. "I've got my nose busted many times, but I ain't never had nobody try to kill me." A joree bird trilled in the bushes: *Tow-heeeeee! Tow-heeeee!* Aidan pondered whether Dobro was exceptionally wise or just a regular feechie scrapper.

"Pantherbane," said Dobro slowly, as if trying the name out. "If it's all right with you, I'm just going to call you Aidan of the Tam. That's who you were when I met you."

"That's who I still am," protested Aidan.

"'Aidan of the Tam I am,'" began Dobro, repeating the song Aidan sang in the bottom pasture the first day they met. "'A liege man true of Darrow.'"

Aidan finished the stanza:
The kingdom's foes I will oppose
With sword and spear and arrow.

"You a liege man true, all right," said Dobro. "Ain't no doubt about that. But I got a question. What if the kingdom's foe turns out to be the king hisself? Who you gonna oppose then?"

Aidan didn't answer. "I'm just saying," continued Dobro, "a king sends the kingdom's best men out to die for no good reason, maybe he ain't much a friend to his own kingdom."

"I'll never oppose my king," Aidan said firmly, in a tone that made it clear he wasn't going to discuss the matter any further.

"That's fine," answered Dobro. "But it looks to me like your king is opposing you. Ain't no cause to get angrified at me."

Aidan's anger subsided. It had been his choice to come to Feechiefen. He had no illusions about King Darrow. Sure, the king believed he was sending Aidan to his death. But it was the king's melancholy, not the true king, that made that decision. Things would be different when he returned to Tambluff Castle with the frog orchid. The king's melancholy would melt away, and things would be as they should be.

Aidan changed the subject. "I've heard stories about he-feechies leaving their family bands to join Chief Larbo's band at Bearhouse. Has anybody from Gergo's band gone over?"

Dobro nodded slowly, his eyes cast down. "Yeah," he said. "Remember Benno Frogger?"

"Yeah," answered Aidan. "Sort of a show-off, if I remember right."

"That's the one," said Dobro. "He picked up and left one day. Said folks in Gergo's band didn't 'preciate him. Since when I was supposed to 'preciate tomfoolery and show-offiness, I don't know, but that's what he said. Said he was going to Bearhouse where a man's free spirit was 'preciated.

"I don't believe poor Benno knew what he was flapping his jaws about. Some strange feechies had been showing up around Bug Neck. I believe he got all that palaver about free spirits and 'preciation from them strangers.

"Benno's mama asked me to run him down, to tell him he was a thick-headed jaybird and drag him home if I had to. I caught up with him and tried to talk sense to him. He just looked at me kind of blank, the way a possum does.

"Then he pulled a knife on me. Not a stone feechie knife, neither, but a cold-shiny knife. I asked him where he got such a thing, and the answer he gave me was mighty peculiar. He said it was a present from the Wilderking."

Chapter Seventeen

Feechiesing

It was well past nightfall when the swamp council convened. A large group of the participants had gone fishing and didn't come back until it was too dark to see what they were doing. Others had spent the late afternoon napping in the island's big oak trees and had to be rousted out.

A cold but satisfying supper of duckweed and duck potatoes was served, and the seventy or so swamp councilors lolled around the smoking village fire for awhile, not saying much. Aidan wondered when they would get down to business.

Hyko stood at last. "We got a lot to talk about tonight," he said, "so I reckon we ought to get this here swamp council started."

"Awww," complained a voice in the crowd. "We just got here!"

"We ain't even had no entertainment yet."

"I just figured," said Hyko, "that we might skip the entertainment tonight and get straight to the confabulation."

A loud and growing grumble arose, and Hyko could see he would have an uprising on his hands if he didn't give in. "All right, all right, all right!" he shouted. "What do you want to do? Fistfights? Contests?"

"How 'bout a feechiesing?" came the voice of Orlo.

A chant rose up from the crowd: "Fee-chie-sing! Fee-chie-sing! Fee-chie-sing!" They stomped in time with the chant. Three sweet gum logs were dragged in and laid side by side to form a small stage called a singstump. Chief Gergo's band, the Bug Neck boys, had a reputation throughout the swamp for putting on the best feechiesings, and the other feechies urged them toward the front.

Branko was the first to mount the singstump. "If it don't make you boys too lonesome for your sweethearts," he began, "I thought I'd sing a little love song." With nods and hoots the audience encouraged him to proceed.

"Sing on," called one of the Coonhouse feechies. "If I can't have my little love-turtle by my side, a love song is the next best thing."

"Sing on!" echoed the rest of the assembly.

Branko clasped his hands over his heart and sang the lilting tones of a feechie love song:

My sweet feechie girl is the swamp's finest pearl—
A treasure, and man, don't I know it.
And I really do think that she loves me, too,
Though she don't always know how to show it.

Her brown eyes are dark like a loblolly's bark.
Her skin is as smooth as a gator.
The one time I kissed her, she knocked me cold, mister.
But nothing could cause me to trade her.

She smells just as sweet as a mud turtle's feet.
Her hair is as soft as a possum.
Once I walked by her side,
    but she knocked me cross-eyed.
It took me a week to uncross 'em.

Her voice is as pleasin' as swamp lily season
She talks kind of froggy and crickety.
Once I give her a rose, and she busted my nose.
My sweetie can be right persnickety.

I'll give you this warning: You mess with my darling,
I'll whop you a right, then a left.
And if that ain't enough, or if you're extra tough,
I might let her whup you herself.

Cheers and applause echoed in the trees. "That was beautiful," called Jerdo. "Gets better every time I hear it."

"If that song don't describe my little Hudu all over . . ." began a member of the Scoggin Mound delegation, but he broke off and dabbed at one eye and then the other with the back of a fist.

"Quick, somebody," called Orlo, "sing something merry, like a hunting song. This feller's done got lonesome for his sweetheart."

"Where's Doyno?" somebody asked. "Doyno, sing the one about your cousin Mungo."

"Yeah, 'Mungo and the Bear,'" shouted another feechie voice. "We ain't heard that one since day before yesterday!"

Doyno, happy to oblige, climbed onto the makeshift singstump and without further ceremony launched into his signature song, a ballad about his relative's epic struggle with a great black bear. Every feechie in the camp knew all the words by heart, but they joined in only on the refrain:

The scrape was fresh upon the tree,
The musk was on the air.
Mungo said, "Boys, follow me—
Let's get ourselves a bear."

We tracked him through the bottomland,
We knowed he wasn't long.
We heard him racketing through the cane
And Mungo egged us on.

Give him chase, boys, give him chase.
Don't let Bruin win the race.
Through the thickets, through the brakes,
Give him chase, boys, give him chase.

He led us where the bamboo spears
Grow dense then denser, densest.
We caught up where the canebrake clears
And where the creek commences.

Old Bruin rared and slashed around
And give a roar like thunder.
We was all ready to lay it down,
But Mungo was a wonder.

Give him chase, boys, give him chase.
Don't let Bruin win the race.
Through the thickets, through the brakes,
Give him chase, boys, give him chase.

There weren't no fear in Mungo's eye.
That feechie was a bold'un.
He only stood about waist-high
To the bear, and yet he told him:

"I want your hide, you ugly bear,
And a necklace from your claws,
A pot of your grease to slick my hair
And steaks for one and all."

Give him chase, boys, give him chase.
Don't let Bruin win the race.
Through the thickets, through the brakes,
Give him chase, boys, give him chase.

He raised his spear behind his ear,
And hollered out, "Let fly!"
Our points rained thick upon the bear
Like hailstones from the sky.

But don't you cry for that old bear.
Spears can't break his stride.
Half he swatted from the air.
The rest bounced off his hide.

Give him chase, boys, give him chase.
Don't let Bruin win the race.
Through the thickets, through the brakes,
Give him chase, boys, give him chase.

So Mungo charged; they did collide,
And here commenced the drama.
Old Bruin stretched his big arms wide
And hugged him like a mama.

The bear mashed Mungo good and thin
And rearranged his stuffin'.
His eyes bulged out, his chest caved in.
(This hug was none too lovin'.)

Give him chase, boys, give him chase.
Don't let Bruin win the race.
Through the thickets, through the brakes,
Give him chase, boys, give him chase.

Mungo managed to free a thumb.
He poked old Bruin's eye.
The bear let go to rub it some,
And Mungo slipped on by.

He clumb up Bruin's brawny rear
And hugged his hairy neck.
Bru bucked and rared and spun and veered,
But Mungo wouldn't shake.

The bear tore out across the swamp
With Mungo in a clench.
The last we saw was Bruin's rump,
And they ain't been back since.

Give him chase, boys, give him chase.
Don't let Bruin win the race.
Through the thickets, through the brakes,
Give him chase, boys, give him chase.

The feechies whooped and cheered and stomped like thunder. Aidan was spellbound. When Doyno dismounted the singstump, Aidan caught him by the arm. "Was that story true?" he asked.

"'Course it's true," answered Doyno. He seemed surprised anyone would question the truth of a feechie ballad. "Happened about five winters ago. I seen the whole thing myself."

"And your cousin Mungo"—Aidan tried to put it as delicately as possible—"what became of him?"

"Can't say I know," answered Doyno in a very matter-of-fact tone. "Somebody said they thought he'd took up with the bear and his family. Said they saw somebody looked a lot like Mungo raiding a bee tree with some bears."

Aidan gave Doyno a doubtful look, but Doyno didn't appear to notice. "I don't believe it though," continued Doyno. "Mungo's so mean and aggravating, I don't reckon any bears would put up with him. Besides," he added, by way of emphasis, "Mungo always stunk something terrible."

By this time the feechies were growing impatient for the next song. "Let's hear something new," called Branko.

"Yeah, something we ain't heard yet," agreed Tombro. "Dobro, you always pirooting around all over the place. I wager you've heard some new ballads."

"Sure, I know a new ballad," answered Dobro. "I learnt it from the beach feechies. But it's terrible sad, and I'm fearsome it would bust up the merriment."

"Sing on, Dobro," encouraged Odo. "The sadder the better. I could use a good cry."

"I don't mind singing it," continued Dobro, "but I ought to warn you, it's terrible long."

"Sing on," shouted a voice from the crowd. "We got nowhere to be."

So Dobro mounted the big singstump. "This here sadballad is called 'The Thing That I Done,'" he explained. Then, as was customary for the singer of a sadballad, he pulled a long face, closed his eyes, and began to sing in a keening voice as high and as lonesome as a tree frog's:

Now listen up children to my tale of woe.
I used to be happy a long time ago.
Now everyone calls me the miserable one.
It's all on account of the thing that I done.

I hope that you'll learn
    from the mistakes I've made.
I hope that you won't play the games that I played.
I done what I done with no thought of tomorrow.
And now I got nothing but mis'ry and sorrow.

Pobo, already primed for a good cry, tuned up at the first mention of misery and woe. By the end of the second stanza, he was leaning on Doyno, his face buried in his hands, wailing as if his best friend had died. After a brief pause, Dobro carried on with his ballad. Such outbursts were to be expected at a feechiesing.

My mama, she learnt me the things I should know.
My daddy, he showed me the way I should go.
But I wouldn't be an obedient son.
I went out and I done the thing that I done.

Now that a mother was involved, there were sniffles all around. A few sobs could be heard in the crowd.

"I miss my mama," wailed Branko. "She's the finest she-feechie ever swung on a vine." Doyno pushed Branko from behind. "She ain't neither," he blubbered. His eyes were red-rimmed from crying for his own mother. "My mama could whup your mama any day!" For a moment it appeared a fistfight was about to break out, but the other feechies shushed Doyno and Branko, anxious to hear what awful thing had ruined the balladeer's life. Soon it was quiet enough for Dobro to continue.

I once was so jolly, but now I just suffer.
Things has got rough, and they'll only get rougher.
My troubles and worries and distress begun
When I did that thing that I shouldn't have done.

Oh, this thing that I done, at the time I enjoyed it.
But listen to me, child, you better avoid it.

It ain't worth the heartache, it ain't worth the strife.
The thing that I done has done ruint my life.

By now the whole swamp council was dissolved in tears. Some had their arms around one another, sobbing on each others' shoulders. Others were laid out flat on the sand, literally wallowing in pity for the poor soul in the ballad whose whole life had collapsed, whose happiness was shattered because of one mistake. They were desperate for more details. What was this one thing that had caused so much heartache? How might they avoid a similar fate? They hung on Dobro's every word.

Lean in here close, and I'll tell you my tale.
It'll straighten your hair, it'll cause you to wail.
But if my sad story can save even one,
I don't mind your knowing this thing that I done.

Except for a few involuntary sobs, the feechies were perfectly silent. All eyes were on Dobro. Their anticipation grew almost unbearable as Dobro launched into a stanza of heartfelt humming, a sort of instrumental interlude: "Hmmm, hmmmm, hmmm, hmmmm, hmmm . . ."

Dobro launched into a second stanza of humming, his eyes still shut tight as if he were lost in the music. But his audience's patience was starting to fray. "Any day now," grumbled a feechie named Beppo.

"Come on, Dobro," whined Branko. "Ain't it time you moved this here story along?"

Dobro just kept humming, but as he moved his head around in time with the music, Aidan thought he saw one eye peep open just enough to get the lay of the land. Then, suddenly, the sadballad broke off, and Dobro sprang from the singstump like a bullfrog and soared over the first row of the audience. He was leaping for a grapevine hanging over Branko's head. But it was a few inches too far. His fingertips just grazed the thick, woody vine and he belly-flopped onto Branko's tortoiseshell helmet with a great, air-expelling *oooooffff.* Dobro and a very surprised Branko both thudded to the ground.

A swarm of feechiefolk was on Dobro in an instant. "Where do you think you're going?" asked Beppo. "You get up and finish that sadballad."

"Put him back on the singstump," somebody shouted. The angry feechies carried Dobro roughly over their heads and deposited him back on the sweet gum logs, where he stood sheepish and silent for a few moments.

"Well?" grumbled Doyno. "Let's hear it."

Dobro closed his eyes, took a deep breath, and began again: "Hmmm, hmmm, hmmm, hmmm . . . hmmm, hmmm, hmmm . . ."

"Confound you!" shouted Branko. "You stop that humming and commence to singing!"

"If you ain't singing real words by the time I count to five . . ." began Beppo.

Somebody butted in. "You can't count to five, Beppo."

"Confound it all!" wailed Dobro. "I done forgot how the sadballad goes."

None of the feechies was crying now. They hemmed Dobro in from either side of the singstump, and they looked ready for a fight.

"How can you remember all them preambulations," asked Hyko, "and forget the main point?"

"You launched into a sadballad called 'The Thing that I Done,'" pointed out Branko, "without you knew the thing that was done."

Dobro looked more sheepish than ever. He now remembered that the one time he heard the sadballad sung, he had fallen asleep before it was over. Now Pobo scrambled onto the singstump to confront Dobro. His dirty face had clean streaks where tears had streamed down. "Do you mean to tell me," Pobo began, "that you got me all wound up, worried sick over that person who done whatever he done, missing my own mama, and generally feeling miserable, for *nothing?*"

Dobro shrugged. "Sorry, Pobo," he said. But Pobo was in no mood for apologies. He lunged for Dobro. Dobro ducked away from him, leaped off the singstump, and bulled his way through the encircling feechies to a nearby beech tree. He shinned up the tree like a squirrel, with hotly pursuing feechies streaming up behind him. But all stopped stock-still, even Dobro, when they realized the treetops were full of strange feechies retreating limb to limb away from them and deeper into the forest.

Chapter Eighteen

A Boat Ride

Aidan scrambled up the nearest water oak to join the pursuit through the treetops. But by the time he made the first leap, the sounds of the chase were far away. He was still a civilizer, after all. No civilizer, not even Pantherbane himself, could tree-walk like a feechie in a chase.

It was a moonless night; clouds had rolled in before dark to obscure even the faint light of the stars. Aidan climbed back down rather than risk further tree walking with no light and no feechies to guide him. He dropped from the lowest limb onto the leaf-strewn ground, just at the edge of the firelight.

Two shadows darted from behind the trees and closed on either shoulder. Aidan felt hot breath at his ears and smelled the unmistakably pungent odor of he-feechies.

"What sort of critter is this?" hissed a voice at his right ear. "He dresses like a feechie, but he wears foot covers like a civilizer." He stepped on Aidan's boot.

"He tries to walk in the treetops like a feechie," whispered the voice at Aidan's left ear, "but he moves like a civilizer." The shadowy figure did an exaggeratedly stiff pantomime of Aidan's cautious movements in the treetop.

"He's got a turtle-shell helmet, but his hair looks like civilizer hair."

"So is he a feechie or a civilizer?"

"I believe he's a feechielizer."

"Whatever he is, I reckon the Wilderking will want to have a look at him."

Aidan saw the glint of two shiny knives in the fading firelight. He opened his mouth to call for help, but a slimy, bony hand clamped over the bottom half of his face. One of his attackers tied his hands behind his back, and the other gagged him with a length of vine. They marched him to a flatboat waiting at the water's edge, then tied his feet, lifted him into the boat, and poled away noiselessly into the blackness of the swamp.

They poled throughout the night. Aidan crouched in the middle of the boat; his captors were at either end. The feechies never spoke a word, and Aidan, being gagged, couldn't speak either. He was alone with his thoughts for an entire sleepless night, wondering what fate awaited him.

At sunup, Aidan finally got a good look at his captors. They had a harder look about them than even the usual run of feechies. The feechie operating the push pole in the stern of the craft was as sharp-featured as a jackfish. His nose, his chin, and even the Adam's apple on his twig-thin neck all came to sharp points. The one sitting in the front had the look of a bottom-feeder. His rounded chin turned downward, taking his mouth with it. Even when he sat straight up, his lips pointed toward the bottom of the boat. His flattened nose had obviously been broken more than once. It meandered down his face like the River Tam itself.

"Sunup," announced the pole-pusher in a raspy voice.

"I ain't blind, Pickro," grumbled Bottom-Feeder. "I can see the sun's up."

"Just making conversation, Carpo," Pickro answered.

But Carpo wouldn't let it rest. "I probably knowed it was sunup before you did."

"How you reckon that?" snarled Pickro.

"'Cause I'm in the front of the boat." Carpo showed all three of his front teeth in a pleased little smile.

"How'd you like to be even farther out in front of the boat?" asked Pickro, lunging to shove Carpo into the water. The boat lurched violently, and Aidan prayed for peace. Bound hand and foot, he didn't like his chances should he get dumped into the Feechiefen.

A gigantic alligator, much longer than the boat, opened its jaws in preparation for an easy breakfast. This had a sobering effect on Pickro, who returned to his post in the stern of the boat.

The flash of anger was over. "You reckon it's safe to float in the daytime?" asked Carpo.

"I reckon so," Pickro answered. "We're a whole night's float from Scoggin Mound. Anybody out looking for this civilizer gots to be behind us. Can't be in front of us. We're better off to keep poling." So they poled on, deeper into the dark heart of the Feechiefen.

Carpo looked back at Pickro. "Breakfast time," he declared. "You hungry?"

"Starving," answered Pickro. "I could eat a civilizer."

Both feechies hee-hawed at this. Even Aidan couldn't help but smile a little, even though he was the butt of the morbid joke.

Carpo seemed impressed with Aidan's sense of humor. "How 'bout you, civilizer?" he asked. "You hungry?" Aidan nodded. Carpo pulled his shiny knife from his belt. Holding it up to the morning light, he admired its gleam almost involuntarily. Then he cut the vine gag so Aidan could eat.

"What you doing?" barked Pickro. "You want him hollering for help?"

Carpo looked in every direction. They were in the deep of the deep swamp. "What's he going to holler?" he asked. Then in a high, mocking voice he called out, "Help! I'm a civilizer! Save me from these mean old feechies!"

Pickro laughed. "You right, Carpo. Even if somebody heard him, they ain't likely to jump in on the civilizer's side, are they?"

When Carpo cut Aidan's wrist bindings, Pickro protested again. "Bless my liver! If you ain't the mollycoddlinest guard I ever seen! He's a prisoner, not a playpretty!"

"Was you planning on feeding him his breakfast like a mama bird?" Carpo retorted. "He can't eat with his hands tied behind his back, can he?" He retied Aidan's hands in the front, an arrangement that Aidan found much more agreeable.

Breakfast was dried duckweed pressed into a flattened mass. Carpo pulled it out of his side pouch and passed it around in palm-sized squares. It wasn't so bad—certainly not the worst feechie food Aidan had ever had. They washed it down with swamp water scooped up in their helmets.

While his captors chewed their breakfast and watched the swamp birds come to life, Aidan thought it was as good a time as any to see if his feechiefriend status would carry any weight with these feechies. He raised his bound hands in a series of elaborate morning stretches, in the hope that either Carpo or Pickro would notice the feechiemark on his forearm. But they just gazed blankly across the water.

Aidan decided to use a more direct approach. After all, they might retie the gag at any time. He might as well talk while he could. "You might not have known it," he said as nonchalantly as he could manage, "but I'm a feechiefriend." Carpo just grunted a little. Pickro said nothing.

Aidan pressed his case. "You know, 'His fights is our fights, and our fights is his'n.'" The silence was deafening. But Aidan kept things rolling. "My feechie name's Pantherbane. You may have heard of me."

"Sure we've heard of you," said Pickro. It was the first time he had spoken directly to Aidan. "I reckon everybody in the swamp's heard of Pantherbane."

At last! thought Aidan. *Now we're getting somewhere.*

"But Pantherbane's pretty old news down at Bearhouse," said Carpo. "Now that we got the Wilderking on the island, we got some new rules. Wilderking give us a whole new way of doing things."

Aidan held out his arms again and nodded at the red alligator scar on his forearm. "Does this feechiemark mean nothing to you?"

"In Larbo's band, we never put much stock in that kind of thing," said Carpo. "Kind of did our own thing, if you know what I mean. When the Wilderking come to us last year, he was real interested in the feechiemark. He told us that if anybody with a feechiemark ever showed up in Feechiefen, we was supposed to bring him back to Bearhouse."

Pickro picked up the story. "Word got around the swamp a few days ago that Pantherbane was going to be at a swamp council at Scoggin Mound. Bunch of us seen the chance to look in on the North Swamp boys and bring the Wilderking his feechiefriend all at the same time."

"This Wilderking," asked Aidan, "where did he come from?"

"Don't know exactly," answered Carpo. "Chief Larbo showed up one day with a civilizer, and he told us he was the Wilderking. We'd all heard about the Wilderking when we was wee-feechies—how a civilizer king would rule over the civilizers and the feechies too. But none of us believed it much anymore."

"Larbo explained how it was all true, and how this here civilizer was the man hisself," said Pickro.

"That made us feel good," explained Carpo. "Larbo's boys ain't always been the best-loved feechies in the swamp, so we was tickled to know the Wilderking come to Bearhouse Island and our little band, to get his Wilderkingdom started."

"He talked so high-flown and smart," said Pickro. "I could listen to the Wilderking talk all day long."

"He give us a whole new way to think about ourselves," added Carpo, "and the swamp too."

"It's like the Wilderking says," Pickro continued, "feechiefolks is good folks, with plenty of good qualities. Loyal, good fighters, we know the woods, got strong backs and a whole heap of energy. But most feechiefolks ain't got the ambition that God gave a salamander.

"But the Wilderking says that with a little gumption and discipline and a commitment to poor grass, we can make something out of ourselves."

Carpo thought about what Pickro had said. "I don't think he said 'poor grass.'"

"Sure he said 'poor grass,'" said Pickro. "Wilderking says it all the time."

"I don't think 'poor grass' is right," Carpo insisted.

"Commitment to progress?" suggested Aidan. "Was he saying commitment to progress?"

"Maybe that's it," conceded Pickro. "Anyway, it's what feechiefolks need. Just look around you." He waved his hand toward a stand of giant cypress. "Lot of folks'd call them trees. The Wilderking calls them natural race horses." He leaned back and watched for the effect of his big words to sink in.

"Natural resources?" asked Aidan.

"Maybe that's it," said Pickro. "But, anyway, you cut a few of them trees down, and a civilizer can build a house out 'em. And here's the best part: Civilizers will trade you gold for a tree!" Pickro cocked an eyebrow at Aidan, judging the impact this revelation might have on the civilizer.

"But what do feechiefolk need with gold?" asked Aidan.

Pickro and Carpo looked at each other for a moment. They had never thought of that before. Finally, Carpo offered a feeble answer: "Because it's shiny! Ain't you never seen gold before?"

A snowy egret glided overhead. Pickro aimed an imaginary crossbow at it and shot. "Plume birds is a natural race horse too. We send plumes to the civilizers, and they give us arrows, spears, knives—not the sorry stone kind like the other feechies use but the kind made out of cold-shiny."

Aidan's eyes narrowed. "What civilizers do you trade with?"

Pickro shrugged his shoulders. "I don't know. The Wilderking knows them. I think some of them live across the ocean."

Pyrthens, thought Aidan. *I knew it.*

Pickro shook his head and chuckled. "Can you believe anybody'd be so thickheaded to trade you cold-shiny for something as useless as a bird feather?"

Carpo spoke in a singsongy voice:
The plumes go out,
The shiny comes in.
Larbo's band
Gonna rise again.

Carpo's eyes gleamed like burnished steel. "And now the Wilderking's got feechies making their own cold-shiny on Bearhouse Island."

"What are you going to do with that much cold-shiny?" asked Aidan.

"We going to rule this swamp," answered Carpo, rubbing his hands together. "That's what we going to do with it."

Carpo and Pickro seemed almost intoxicated by the idea of that much power. They couldn't keep it a secret. "The other feechie bands is going to find out what the Bearhouse boys is made of," said Pickro. He pounded his chest.

"They not gonna hold their head so high," added Carpo.

"And then," whispered Pickro, as if someone might overhear, "after the Wilderking makes Larbo the king of the Feechiefen, a whole army of feechies gonna march on the civilizers."

"Pickro, I don't think we're supposed to be telling folks about that," warned Carpo. "Especially not civilizers."

"Who's he going to tell?" asked Pickro. "He ain't never gonna leave Bearhouse Island. Anyway," he continued, "Wilderking says the civilizers is gone soft. Says they couldn't stand up to a real feechie army."

"You seen what we done to them foreign civilizers at the Eechihoolee," said Carpo. "And that was without no training or cold-shiny. Wilderking says that was the powerfullest civilizer army in the world we whupped."

"He told you true," said Aidan, but he wasn't thinking about the Eechihoolee. He was wondering whether he could stop the lunatic posing as the Wilderking.

Chapter Nineteen

Bearhouse Island

plume of thick black smoke billowed up over the southern horizon. "There it is!" whooped Carpo. "There's Bearhouse."

"What's that fire?" Aidan asked.

"That fire," said Pickro, "is poor grass."

"Progress," Aidan corrected.

Pickro nodded. "You sure got that right!"

They were four days' poling from Scoggin Mound. And though Aidan's stomach churned with dread at the thought of being handed over to Chief Larbo and the pretended Wilderking, he could take some consolation in the fact that at least he wouldn't have to spend another day in the boat with these two yahoos. *I don't want to see another flatboat as long as I live,* he thought. But he took back his wish when he considered the possibility that he actually might not live to see another flatboat.

Pickro poled faster, like a horse headed back for the stall. *"Hoooo-weee!"* he yodeled. "Ain't Chief Larbo and the Wilderking gonna be proud of us, bringing Pantherbane hisself to Bearhouse!"

"Hey, Pantherbane," said Carpo. "You reckon you could growl and make ugly faces when we get out the boat? Maybe kick at us and flop around and show your toothies?"

"It might be kinda disappointing to the boys, you know, if you was to come in all polite and peaceful," Pickro explained. "It'd just look a little better if you was to act more like a dangerous prisoner."

"And since you gonna get throwed in jail either way, Pantherbane," said Carpo, "we didn't figure you'd mind putting on a show for the boys." Aidan rolled his eyes. He would be very, very glad to get out of this boat.

They could hear Bearhouse before they could see it. The hammer and clang of metalwork was jarring to Aidan's ears here in the depths of the Feechiefen. For days, the background noises had been birds, frogs, and bugs with the occasional splash of a fish or alligator, nearly drowned out by the constant, inane chatter of Carpo and Pickro. But Bearhouse sounded like one big blacksmith shop. *Clang! Clank! Screeeeee!* And the steady rhythm of axes. *Chuck! Chuck! Chuck!* And the creak and snap and thunder of falling trees.

When Bearhouse at last came into view, Aidan's heart sank. The north end of the island rose from the black water like the top of a great bald, scarred head. Most of the trees were gone, and the ground cover too. The sun glared down with a punishing brightness on the feechies who scurried to and fro across the bare sand.

"Where are the trees?" Aidan asked.

"Trees fire the forges," answered Pickro. "Forges makes the swords and spears and axes."

"You're feechies," Aidan said. "Surely you miss the trees, and the animals that lived here."

Carpo shrugged. "Trees is nice. Critters is nice. But it's like the Wilderking says, once we whup all the other bands in this swamp, we'll have all the trees and critters we want."

"Is the whole island cleared?" Aidan asked. "Is the whole forest gone?"

"Naw, naw," said Pickro in a reassuring tone. "We ain't got around to chopping out the south half of the island." He whistled. "But you talk about natural race horses!"

"Wilderking aims to start a new shiny-works down at Round Pond on the south end," gushed Pickro. "And we gonna be able to make more cold-shiny than you ever seen!"

"We'll use the pond for the cooling pool, and them big oak trees is perfect for the forge fires," Carpo added.

"Oak burns hot," Pickro explained. He waved dismissively at the trees around him. "Not like these cypresses."

To the right, a larger flatboat was headed west, away from the island. "There goes more plume bales!" shouted Carpo.

Pickro pointed eagerly at another boat coming the opposite way, toward the island. It was an identical boat, but it rode much lower in the water. "Hee-haw!" the sharp-faced feechie cried. "More cold-shiny!" He broke into song:

The plumes go out,
The shiny comes in.
Larbo's band
Gonna rise again.

They were very close now to the landing in the northern corner of the island. No birds flew overhead. No fish disturbed the surface of the water. No frogs peeped from the maiden cane that managed to survive at the water's edge. There weren't even alligators in the water here at Bearhouse. The place was dead, except for the feechies who hurried back and forth.

Pickro poled the boat to the landing, and Carpo pulled Aidan from the boat by his tied hands. Looking very important and self-satisfied, they marched Aidan across the bare sand. The bustling little village stood still as they paraded through. Feechie blacksmiths in gator-hide aprons held their hammers aloft in midblow and turned their soot-blackened faces to follow the civilizer. Forge fires cooled as bellows-tenders stopped their work and gawked.

Aidan's captors prodded him across the settlement to a wooden stockade surrounded by a palisade of upended pine logs sharpened at the top. There was a door in the wall facing the settlement, and beside the door stood two guards.

The guards were civilizers, the first civilizers Aidan had seen since Massey left him at the south bank of the Tam. They were short, broad, and well armed. "This here civilizer is Pantherbane," Pickro announced to the guards. He gave them a second to be impressed by this information. "We brung him to the Wilderking."

One of the guards ducked through the door into the fort. Carpo called after him, "Tell him it was Carpo and Pickro what captured him." He winked broadly at Pickro and rocked up and down on his feet in smug self-regard.

The guard returned shortly. "The Wilderking says to take the prisoner to the holding cage. His Majesty will see the prisoner in his own time." Carpo and Pickro were dejected. They turned to go, and Pickro called over his shoulder, "Make sure he knows it was Carpo and Pickro what brung him."

Aidan's guards marched him back to the northern edge of the island and into a cage made of thick bamboo poles. They locked the door with a crude iron padlock. The sun drilled down on Aidan. There was no shade, nothing to sit or lie on besides the bare ground. There was nothing to do but wait and watch. He waited all day, and the Wilderking never came.

Aidan spent the long day observing the scene around him. Behind his cage was the open swamp. In front was the feechie settlement. From where Aidan sat, he could see five different forges burning. Blacksmiths took the bars of iron that arrived on flatboats and pounded the metal into arms and armor. Some of it they pounded into more mundane implements, such as shovels and picks. Feechies scuttled back and forth with wheelbarrows, carrying finished armaments from the forges to the Wilderking's stockade, carrying unfinished metal from the landing to the forges. Feechie timber crews went back and forth, sometimes with axes over their shoulders, sometimes lugging chunks of firewood to fuel the forges.

Aidan had never seen feechies look so busy. He had never seen feechies look so tired. And another thing occurred to Aidan. He had never before seen feechiefolk look so frightened. Every half hour or so, the door to the stockade swung open, and a pair of civilizer taskmasters came out. When they walked around the settlement, the feechies always started moving faster.

On Aidan's second day in the cage, Pickro and Carpo came back. To Aidan's horror, they had been assigned to be his jailers. It was like being in the flatboat all over again, with their incessant yammering. Aidan wondered if this was a cruel punishment the false Wilderking had devised for him. When they arrived at their posts beside the cage door, they were already deep into a conversation about what they were going to do after the Wilderking established himself as king of Corenwald.

"I ain't raising none of them smelly sheep," Carpo was saying, "but I might could get used to riding around on a horse. I'll howdy all the pretty civilizer ladies, and they'll howdy me. They'll say, 'Howdy, Mr. Carpo. How you come on this morning?' and I'll say, 'Pretty tolerable good, pretty lady, except I got a bad case of the burps.' And the lady'll say, 'You poor feller. I get the same way sometimes, but I eat a bait of latherleaf, and it mostly goes away.'"

Aidan groaned. "I promise you, that's not what a civilizer lady would say."

"What do you know about it?" asked Pickro.

"He's just mad 'cause his folks ain't gonna be in charge no more," said Carpo. Aidan retreated to the back of his cage, away from the two feechies.

"I reckon I know what kind of house I'm gonna get," Pickro announced. "I seen a great big civilizer house on the river, up on a bluff of honey-color sandstone. Right where the river bends around. Biggest thing I ever seen. It was made of sandstones piled up on each other. And it had a little creek in the front where you can keep your alligators if you get lonesome for the swamp."

Aidan was trying to ignore the feechies, but he couldn't help himself. "Tambluff Castle?" he blurted. "You want to live in Tambluff Castle?" He threw his hands in the air. "Let's just say this impostor Wilderking does overthrow King Darrow and makes himself king of Corenwald. Do you really think he's going to set you up with big houses and big estates? If he brings you to Tambluff, it will only be to get more work out of you."

He swept his hand in a broad gesture. "Look at this place. Do you really think this is how the true Wilderking would do things? There's no wilderness here. The trees are gone. The birds are gone. You can hardly breathe for the smoke." He pointed at a group of feechies shuffling past with shovels over their shoulders. "Look at them! Look at you! You were a free and happy people before this Wilderking came along. He's made you slaves. Not with chains but with empty promises of power and riches and ease." He nodded his head toward the nearest forge, where sweating feechies were heaving big chunks of wood onto the fire. "Is this really the way you want to live?"

Aidan shook his head. "Don't you understand? This pretended Wilderking has wiggled into the worst part of your nature, and he's enslaved you. That's not how the real Wilderking is going to do it."

The feechies stared at Aidan, astonished by his outburst. They seemed to be considering what Aidan had said. But Pickro spoke at last. "Don't listen to him, Carpo. He's just jealous."

"Just jealous," repeated Carpo. "It's like the Wilderking says: Civilizers ain't gonna like it when feechiefolks come to get what's ours."

"That's right," Pickro added. "Wilderking says you civilizers think us feechiefolks is second-class sun-setters. But we ain't." Pickro folded his arms in the gesture of a man who has made his point. Aidan squinted at him, trying to make some sense of what the feechie had said.

"I don't think he said 'second-class sun-setters,'" said Carpo. "I think he said 'second-class setter-suns.'"

Aidan blinked, still confused. Then a light dawned at last, and he couldn't help laughing. "Second-class citizens," he said. "The civilizers think you're second-class citizens."

"See?" said Pickro to his partner. "He don't even deny it."

‡ ‡ ‡

Aidan's second day in the cage went much like his first, except that the ceaseless, idiotic chatter of Pickro and Carpo was layered on top of the monotony and misery of being locked in an unshaded cage in the middle of a swamp. Aidan paced back and forth to keep his blood flowing, and he watched the dull-eyed feechies go about their daily labors. He watched smoke billow and curl in black violation of the Feechiefen sky. He saw plume hunters arrive with their hateful trophies and another plume bale go out toward the world of the civilizers.

But he still didn't see the man who called himself the Wilderking.

The third day was very much like the second. The tedium and the sun's unremitting glare, however, were starting to do their work on Aidan. He didn't feel like pacing that day but instead lay in the back corner of his cage watching the sun make its way across the sky. The conversation of a new pair of guards sounded to Aidan more like the buzzing of wasps than intelligible speech. He left his duckweed cakes untouched and didn't drink much of the water his captors provided.

Aidan didn't even seem to notice that night had fallen or that Pickro and Carpo were back on post. He drifted into a fitful sleep that didn't seem very different from the dull waking of the daytime. His dreams were confused and vivid. Calling out in his sleep, he spoke many more words than he had in the whole previous day.

The feechie settlement was midnight-still when Aidan began to awaken. A first-quarter moon hung high in a clear sky, spilling its silver light across the sandy desolation of Bearhouse Island. Aidan was startled out of a dreamy half sleep when he caught a glimpse of a white cloud hovering like a phantom just outside his cage. When his eyes adjusted, he saw that the cloud was a spray of egret plumes. It was a headdress, worn by a man—a civilizer, judging by his size—who crouched a few feet away. Aidan knew at once that, unless he was still dreaming, this had to be the false Wilderking watching him sleep.

"Who are you?" Aidan asked.

The visitor answered in a whisper. "I am you."

"I am you?" scoffed Aidan. "Nobody talks like that."

"All right then," continued the stranger, still whispering. "I am what you might have been if you hadn't been so stupid."

Aidan tried to get a look at the stranger's face, but the night was dark and his face was mostly obscured by the egret plumes anyway. The headdress seemed to glow with its own light, but it didn't illuminate its wearer's face.

"I am the Wilderking," the stranger continued. "The boss of this swamp, as the feechiefolk say. And before long I'll be the boss of all Corenwald."

Aidan strained to hear any trace of a Pyrthen accent—indeed, any clue to where this impostor had come from. But any such clues disappeared in the whispered speech.

"You could have so easily been where I am," the pretender continued. "But you didn't seize your chance when you had it. That's the only real difference between you and me." He shook his head, and the egret plumes waved extravagantly. "After Bonifay, you had a lot of people convinced you were the Wilderking—civilizer and feechie alike. But you frittered it away. Did you think somebody was just going to hand you the kingdom?" He snorted a short, mean laugh. "And now it's too late. Your moment's past."

Aidan racked his brain. A courtier? Was this someone he knew from King Darrow's court? "You know a lot about me," he said.

"I have made you my study," the false Wilderking hissed back. With that, he left and made his way back to the stockade. Aidan lay listening to the raucous snoring of Pickro and Carpo, whose sleep was undisturbed. It wasn't long before Aidan joined them in sleep. He dreamed of feechiefolk in Tambluff Castle.

Chapter Twenty

Fracas

While Aidan was trying to eat his breakfast the next morning, a fist-sized rock came sailing into Pickro's helmet. *Thwack!* He slumped into a pile in front of Aidan's cage. Pickro had scarcely hit the ground before Dobro Turtlebane whirled in like a tornado from behind the one tree remaining on the north end of the island. He snatched Pickro's spear from the ground and cracked the butt across Carpo's helmet. Carpo, too, dropped to the ground before he realized what was happening.

Dobro rattled the cage door, looking to make a quick getaway with Aidan. But he had never seen a padlock before—he had hardly ever seen a door—and he didn't understand why the door wouldn't open. "I'm gonna get you outta this cage," he said, breathing hard. "I'm gonna get you out."

Four Bearhouse feechies patrolling nearby heard the commotion. They saw their comrades lying motionless on the ground and a strange feechie trying to open the civilizer's cage. They started running for Dobro.

"Ooook!" their leader barked. "What do you think you're doing?"

"It's locked!" Aidan shouted at Dobro. "It won't open. Run away!"

But Dobro didn't run away. He kept rattling the lock, pushing and pulling against the door that wouldn't budge.

"I shouldn'ta left you at Scoggin Mound," he kept repeating. "I shouldn'ta left you!"

"It doesn't matter, Dobro. Run!"

The feechie patrol had Dobro surrounded, but Dobro paid no mind. He worried the lock and rattled the door, as single-minded as a raccoon. Cold-shiny spearpoints gleamed all around him, but he paid no mind.

The lead feechie gave the signal, and all four patrollers attacked. Preferring to capture him alive, they flipped their spears around and struck Dobro with the handles rather than the spearpoints. Dobro soon lay battered on the ground, unable or unwilling to rise.

The lead feechie was about to ask Aidan a question when the still, black water behind the cage erupted in a frothing tumult. A hundred feechies from the North Swamp had been lying beneath the surface since before daylight, breathing through reeds, and now they lurched up as one and charged, dripping clubs in hand, on the unsuspecting Bearhouse feechies.

They overwhelmed Dobro's four attackers in short order, but the alarm went out across the island, and two hundred Bearhouse feechies answered the call. They came with swords, spears, and axes, all of shining steel. Their bowmen notched steel-tipped arrows to their bowstrings and pulled them tight. They laughed cruelly at the stocks and clubs of the North Swamp feechies; old-fashioned weapons had no place in the new world ushered in by their Wilderking.

But the North Swamp feechies were undaunted. They formed a line and faced their adversaries without flinching. The air crackled with tension as the two ferocious armies glared at each other across the clearing.

Behind the line of Bearhouse feechies, the door to the stockade swung on its hinges, and Aidan got his second look at the man who claimed to be the Wilderking. Stepping into the morning sunlight, he was a dazzling sight. A long robe of fuzzy white egret plumes trailed behind him, and around his head, egret plumes shot out in all directions like the rays of a fuzzy sun in the headdress he had worn the night before. Even in the daylight, the false Wilderking's face was more or less obscured by the plumage. Beside him stood an old feechie in a wolfhide cape—Chief Larbo, Aidan figured. Six thick-bodied civilizers, his bodyguard, formed a protective semicircle.

With a clear voice the false Wilderking addressed the Bearhouse feechies: "For this I have trained you, my hearties. You are strong of arm and strong of heart. Your steel is strong too." He raised a plumed spear above his head. "For Bearhouse! For Larbo! For the Wilderking!"

The North Swamp feechies braced for the onslaught. But before it came, a wild cry echoed across the clearing:

Ha-ha-ha-hrawffff-wooooooooo. . . Ha-ha-ha-hrawffff-wooooooooo.

All eyes turned to the bamboo cage from which the watch-out bark had come. Aidan stood with his face pressed between the poles of his cage. Chief Larbo's voice was the first to break the silence. "A watch-out bark!" he called across the battleground. He glanced at the spearheads and arrowpoints glinting all around. "If you don't mind my saying, young civilizer, it looks to me like you the one ought to watch out." The Bearhouse feechies snickered.

"That may be," answered Aidan. "But you'd better watch out too. All of you." The authority in Aidan's voice captivated the attention of every feechie within earshot. "Things will never be the same if you turn those cold-shiny weapons on other feechies."

"That's what I know!" shouted one of the Bearhouse feechies. "Larbo's boys gonna rise again!" A rumble of agreement rose among the Bearhouse feechies, punctuated by two or three enthusiastic whoops.

But Aidan's voice silenced the crowd with a single word: "No!"

All eyes were once again on the civilizer's cage. "If you win this battle for this pretended Wilderking, no feechie will ever rule in this swamp again."

The false Wilderking's plumage shook with rage, and he began to speak: "This fool has—" But a glance from Chief Larbo silenced him, and Aidan went on.

"If you turn a cold-shiny weapon on another feechie, you won't be just killing a feechie. You'll be killing all feechiedom."

The Bearhouse feechies had been foolish, but they weren't altogether stupid. They were listening to Aidan now.

"Today you have a choice to make." Aidan waved his hand in a sweeping gesture to indicate all of Bearhouse Island—the forges, the desolate landscape, the Wilderking's stockade. "Choose this, and you can never go back to the life you lived in your home band. You can't have both."

Aidan noticed that the forest of spears across the battleground were held a little lower. He pressed his advantage. "And you're not just choosing for yourself. You're choosing for the mamas and sweethearts you left behind. You're choosing for your daddies and your granddaddies, for the wee-feechies who can't choose for themselves."

Aidan looked into the silent faces of the Bearhouse feechies. "That's all I have to say."

In their training, the Bearhouse feechies had used their swords and spears to do all sorts of horrible things to fake enemies stuffed with graybeard moss. But now that real enemies were in front of them, they looked more like cousins and former bandmates than enemies. It's not that they minded attacking the invaders. North Swamp boys had no business, after all, on Bearhouse Island. But how much fun could it be to cut them up with cold-shiny weapons?

The Bearhouse feechies threw down their swords, spears, and bows. The North Swamp feechies threw down their clubs. And the two lines rushed headlong toward one another with flying fists, flying feet, and flying leaps. The Battle of Bearhouse was on, and it was ferocious. Aidan had witnessed a few feechie fights.

There was nothing in the civilizer world to compare to a feechie fight for sheer brutishness. Fighting bears would be more civil. The Battle of Bearhouse was a hundred such fights, raging in every direction.

Aidan hung from his cage poles, whipped into a frenzy by the fracas around him. On one hand, he longed to get at the impostor who had tricked and enslaved the Bearhouse feechies. On the other hand, he was thankful for the protection afforded by his bamboo cage. He did his best to cheer the North Swamp boys, but it was hard to tell who was who.

Across the way, Aidan could see the false Wilderking dancing with rage. "You fools!" he screamed over the din of the battle. "Strike! Kill!" Every jerk of his head, every twist of his body was so magnified by his elaborate costume that the figure he cut was more comic than commanding. Larbo, seeing that the battle was being fought the old feechie way, couldn't resist and left the Wilderking's side to join the fun. The bodyguards, on the other hand, stood as if their feet were glued to the sand. They were confused and terrified by the feechies' primal ferocity. The civilizers had weapons, and they didn't mind using them, but they had underestimated what feechies could do in a free fight.

The battle raged. Feechies flew through the air, some leaping to the attack, others being thrown and flipped by their adversaries. In several cases, Aidan noticed that both of the combatants in a hand-to-hand fight were Bearhouse feechies. Because they outnumbered the North Swamp boys, there weren't enough opponents to go around. Some of the Bearhouse feechies had to fight one another—the way girls at a ball sometimes danced with one another when there weren't enough boys. As the battle swirled around him, Aidan noticed a new light in the Bearhouse feechies' eyes. The old, fiery feechie spirit had chased away the dullness born of overwork and a love of cold-shiny. Their swampy exuberance made them more formidable enemies than their flashing weapons ever could.

Dobro Turtlebane, recovered from his earlier setback, now tangled with an unusually large feechie wearing an alligator-claw necklace. And things weren't going well for Dobro. The Bearhouse feechie lifted Dobro over his head and hurled him against Aidan's cage with such force that the whole structure collapsed in a heap. Aidan went to the ground, covering his head against the falling poles, and Dobro landed beside him with a thud and a clatter. He rolled over and moaned. "See, Aidan?" he groaned, holding his ribs. "I told you I'd get you out of this cage."

Aidan spied the false Wilderking across the way. He was still stomping, raging, and waving his arms. Aidan rose to his feet and started walking a straight line toward him. Fists and feet and feechies flew all around him, but on he walked, driven by a single purpose. He stared unblinking at the gyrating, gesticulating fraud, stalking closer, closer, yet the Wilderking was too self-absorbed to notice. Some of the feechies noticed, however, when Aidan stooped to pick up a discarded club. Hyko left off his combat and fell in step behind Aidan, and so did Pobo, Orlo, Tombro, and Odo Watersnake from Chief

Gergo's band. Even Dobro joined in as best he could, limping and holding his ribs.

Aidan was thirty strides away when the Wilderking's bodyguards hustled him inside the stockade. They drew their swords and waited for Aidan and his following. But Aidan kept coming, undeterred, and his following grew. The guards were well armed. But they could count, and it was obvious that they couldn't hold back what was quickly growing into a feechie mob. They, too, retired to the safety of the stockade.

Still Aidan kept coming. His step was quicker now. When he arrived at the stockade door, he raised his club high and brought it down on the doorframe with all his might. *Thwack!*

"I am Aidan Errolson of Longleaf Manor."

Thwack!

"I have come for the impostor who calls himself the Wilderking!"

Thwack!

"I am Pantherbane!"

Thwack!

"You have enslaved a free and happy people!"

Thwack!

"You have defaced this swamp, God's creation!"

Thwack!

"You are a liar!"

Thwack!

"You are a fraud!"

Thwack!

"You are a coward!"

Thwack!

The feechie battle had stopped altogether by the final time Aidan struck his club. All eyes were on Pantherbane at the door of the stockade.

The long silence was broken at last by the voice of the Wilderking, not quite as clear as before, from inside the wooden walls. "Take care you do not talk yourself to death, Pantherbane. You meddler. You ignoramus."

This was what everyone was waiting for. "Rudeswap!" called Chief Larbo. "The Wilderking finished the rudeswap!"

"Hee-haw!" called a feechie voice. "We gonna see a civilizer fight!"

The feechies—North Swamp and Bearhouse alike—stampeded toward the stockade.

"Do you hear that, Wilderking?" shouted Aidan over the confusion. "Your subjects await you." The feechies surrounded the stockade, bruised and bloodied from battle. But there was no response from inside. Dobro, who stood at Aidan's right hand, rapped his knuckles on his helmet, one fist, then the other in a steady rhythm: *Tock . . . Tock . . . Tock . . . Tock . . .*

The feechies around him joined in. *Tock . . . Tock . . . Tock . . . Tock . . .* The tempo was like a great clock ticking out the seconds toward a showdown between Pantherbane and the man who called himself the Wilderking. Fighting out a rudeswap was the most basic point of honor in the Feechie Code. Every second the king remained in the stockade, every second he refused to fight out his rudeswap, his power over the Bearhouse feechies dissolved a little more. Now all of the feechies were pounding their helmets with a deafening urgency: *Tock . . . Tock . . . Tock . . . Tock . . .*

At last the stockade door cracked open. The helmet banging stopped, and the feechies waited eagerly, expectantly for the Wilderking to appear and do his duty. But the man who stepped out of the door wasn't the Wilderking. He was Lawmer, the Wilderking's big, thick-necked lieutenant. He read from a piece of paper:

To tussle with a common ruffian is beneath
the dignity of your king.

There was a general grumble among the feechies, but Lawmer continued.

The Wilderking desires you, his subjects,
to continue with the battle and drive the
invaders off the island. He will address
you when your task is complete.

Chief Larbo was livid. He hopped in a circle around Lawmer, who did his best to maintain a dignified indifference. "Beneath his dignity?" the old feechie barked. "I tell you what's beneath his dignity: hiding from a free fight like a bunny in a brush pile!" He snorted. "Beneath his dignity! I don't care who he is. He swaps rude with a man, he better be ready to fight it out!" Larbo darted behind the big civilizer to push through the stockade door. He meant to have it out face to face with the

Wilderking. Lawmer, quick as a cat, struck Larbo across the back with the flat of his sword. The feechie chieftan sprawled to the ground.

That was the blow that ended the reign of the false Wilderking on Bearhouse Island. The sight of a civilizer striking down a feechie was like a shot of cold water in the faces of the Bearhouse feechies. It jolted them out of their shiny-hungry daze and demolished the last remnants of the false Wilderking's hold over their conscience. The atmosphere was thick with their anger, like the air before a summer storm. Lawmer felt it down his whole spine. He ducked through the door and barricaded it behind him.

The feechie storm broke with terrifying suddenness. Feechies closed on the stockade and climbed the palisades elbow to elbow, one right behind the other. Pobo Sands and Orlo Sands led the way, one on either side of the stockade. Feechies swarmed over the palisades like ants on an anthill. Before the first climbers reached the sharpened tops of the poles, the whole structure began to sway beneath their weight. The stockade had been built by feechie hands, and being the first wooden structure they had ever built, it wasn't very sturdy.

The stockade collapsed on itself in a jumble of falling poles and tumbling feechies. The civilizers were as exposed as soft, pink crawfish that had shed their shells. They flailed about them with their gleaming weapons, and several feechies fell. But it was only a matter of seconds before they were swarmed under by the very people they had lorded over for two long years.

But the Wilderking somehow slipped away from the melee. A flash of white at the edge of the clearing caught Aidan's eye. He saw the robe of egret plumes drop to the ground, and a tall civilizer in boots and tunic, now unencumbered by the trappings of the Wilderking, disappeared into the woods.

Chapter Twenty-one

Revelation

The false Wilderking ran south, toward the end of the island he and Larbo's band had not yet ravaged. Aidan picked up a bodyguard's sword and plunged into the forest after him. The ground on Bearhouse Island gave rise to a riot of vines and entangling brambles. Aidan tried to hack his way through with the sword, but there was little use.

The Wilderking had obviously taken a hidden trail. Aidan couldn't find a path. So he tucked the sword in his belt and climbed a nearby tree. Through the treetops he swung and soared, watching the forest floor for any sign of movement. He was within sight of the island's edge when he saw a rustling in the bushes below. Then, above a stand of sparkleberry bushes, a clump of brown, curly hair appeared.

Swift and light as a bobcat, Aidan tree-walked toward his prey. The Wilderking had made it to the shoreline. A flatboat was waiting for him at the water's edge. That's when Aidan crashed down on him from the treetops. The impostor fell hard onto his face. Aidan scrambled to his feet and stood over his prostrate enemy, sword raised and ready to strike if need be. But the Wilderking made no sudden moves. He hardly moved at all.

"Turn around!" Aidan ordered. "Look at my face."

The man who called himself the Wilderking turned his head slowly to the side, then lifted one shoulder to face his conqueror.

Aidan peered into the narrowed eyes of his enemy, and his face turned white. He had known those eyes since the day he was born. Those eyes had watched Aidan grow up. Aidan had seen those eyes sparkle with laughter many years before. He felt his head grow light. "Maynard," he whispered.

The impostor twisted his mouth into a sneering smile. "Hello, little brother."

Aidan staggered back a step. The sword hung by his side, loose in his grip. "I don't understand."

"Of course you don't understand," Maynard snarled. "How could you understand a man going out and getting what nobody meant to give him? You've never had to work for anything. You've been given everything you've ever had. How could you understand?"

Aidan stood blinking. He couldn't begin to make sense of what was happening.

"You don't know what it's like to be a second son," Maynard continued. It seemed he had practiced this speech many times to himself. "To come so close to being the heir to Longleaf Manor, but instead to spend a lifetime knowing that Brennus is going to get it, that self-satisfied moron, because he was born fifteen months before you were.

"That's bad enough. But then a lunatic shows up pretending to be a prophet and convinces everybody that your baby brother is the Wilderking." He waved a hand dismissively at Aidan. "You! The Wilderking!" He barked one short syllable of a laugh. "The fifth son! That was the last act." Maynard pushed up from his elbow and rose to his feet, looking Aidan in the face. "I wish you'd explain one thing to me: How do you deserve to be the Wilderking more than I do? That's one thing I don't understand."

Aidan didn't answer. He couldn't answer. Maynard's diatribe went on. "Then I saw what the feechiefolk did to the Pyrthens in the Eechihoolee Forest. I realized that if I could train them, arm them, I wouldn't have to depend on any half-wit prophet to make me the Wilderking." He shook his head slowly, condescendingly at Aidan. "Where did you think I'd been these two years?"

Aidan spoke at last. "You have broken Father's heart."

Maynard's smug little smile cracked for a second, but he recovered himself. "Father doesn't have a heart." Then he added, more quietly, "Not for me."

The two brothers stared at each other: the future Wilderking and the false Wilderking. A realization dawned on Aidan. "You wrote the letter to King Darrow, didn't you?"

Maynard laughed out loud. "Of course I did! One of my plume hunters dropped it in the mail wagon."

Now Aidan was the one smiling. "It was your letter, you know, that made King Darrow send me to the Feechiefen."

The irony wasn't lost on Maynard. His scheme to destroy Aidan had instead destroyed his own little kingdom. But he merely shrugged. He gestured at the sword in Aidan's hand. "So are you going to stab me? Run me through? Cut me into little pieces?" Maynard stood with outstretched arms, baring himself to his brother's sword. Aidan didn't raise his hand. Maynard snorted. "I didn't think so." He turned toward the water, stepped into the boat, and began to pole away.

Aidan stepped to the water's edge. "But, Maynard," he called after him, "how did you do it?"

Maynard laughed his mean laugh. "Ask your feechie friend," he called back. "Ask Dobro."

Aidan stood at the verge of the island and watched his brother disappear around the buttress of a cypress tree. He didn't move, just stared at the upside-down world reflected in the black water. He was so confused. His dead brother was alive. And yet it didn't seem like good news. He thought of his father, who was so nearly broken by Maynard's death. What would it do to him if he ever found out about Maynard's life, the wickedness to which he had applied his energies these last two years? Maynard could hardly have hatched a scheme better suited to hurt his family, to violate everything Father had taught his sons about the responsibilities of Corenwalder nobles. But one question kept nagging Aidan: Was this all his fault? It was Aidan, after all, who planted the seed of this scheme in Maynard's head. Maynard would have never believed feechiefolk existed if it weren't for Aidan.

Aidan turned and ran into the forest. Low-hanging boughs closed above his head, blocking out the light and making it impossible for Aidan to tell east from west, north from south. But Aidan didn't care. Ground vines reached up and slung him to the forest floor time and again. But he staggered on, unseeing. He pushed through thorny thickets, unmindful of the briars that raked across his bare chest and back. He sweated off the gray mud that had been his only protection from the vicious insects of the Feechiefen. But he didn't even swat at the bugs or slap at their stings. He was too confused and grief-stricken to care. For hours he blundered in the forest on the south end of Bearhouse. He was broken, bleeding, lost—both inside and outside. He couldn't even remember how to pray.

Then he blundered into a clearing. He stood on the sandy bank of a blackwater pond, a lagoon in the middle of the island. Huge live oaks, hundreds of years old, sprawled their sturdy branches over Aidan's head. Their beards of gray moss nodded reassuringly in the gentle breeze. The birds that roosted in their tops had begun their warbling evensong.

The pond was a perfect circle, a little spot of order and symmetry in the teeming, chaotic wildness of Bearhouse. This, Aidan realized, was Round Pond that Carpo and Pickro had spoken of, the planned site of a new, bigger forge that would use the pond for a cooling pool and the great oak trees to feed the fires. He rejoiced that this place of tranquility and beauty had been rescued from his brother. He threw back his head to gaze high into the crowns of the overarching trees. The most beautiful white flowers he had ever seen were suspended in mid-air, soaring from branch to branch. And Aidan remembered what had brought him to Feechiefen in the first place.

Here was the spot described in the Frog Orchid Chant, where oak trees bordered a perfectly black and perfectly round pond.

In deepest swamp, the house of bears,
An orchid in the spring appears
On oaken limb around a pond
As black as night and round as sun.
It floats in air, a ghostly white.
It soars and leaps like frog in flight.
And in the orchid's essence pure
Is melancholy's surest cure.

Each orchid was a dazzling white, its wide mouth and three petals forming a body about the size of a bullfrog. And from that main body, two long streamers dangled, long and bent like the legs of a leaping frog. They grew on long stems arching from the high branches of the live oaks. When the breeze blew, the frog orchids bobbed up and down in midair like leaping frogs, their long legs coiling and stretching with the motion.

There were hundreds of them in the treetops, a whole squadron of frogs flying through the evening air. Aidan laughed for the joy of the frog orchids. He cried, too, for their beauty. His melancholy was cured. And a prayer was answered that he hadn't been able to pray.

Chapter Twenty-two

The Way Back

The next day, the feechies lit the Bearhouse forge fires again. But this was the last time. They fanned the fires to a white heat only so they could melt their cold-shiny weapons and implements back to raw, unformed metal. North Swamp feechies and Bearhouse feechies alike spent a festive day throwing things into the fire and watching them burn—steel swords and axes, arrows and spears, iron shovels and hammers, padlocks and hinges— anything made of cold-shiny.

They planned a big fire jumping for that evening, but Aidan was anxious to leave. He had King Darrow's frog orchid, still attached to the tree limb it grew on, and he didn't want to wait a day longer than he had to, lest the orchid not survive the trip.

The feechies left the forge fires long enough to see Aidan off. He was nearly senseless from the head butting by the time he actually made it to the landing. Before stepping into the boat, Aidan sought out Orlo and Pobo, who no longer answered to the name of Sands. Their heroics leading the attack on the false Wilderking's palisades had earned them last names. "Orlo Polejumble," Aidan intoned with exaggerated dignity, "Pobo Smashpine." He bowed deeply. "I am pleased to make your acquaintance."

Tombro, Hyko, and the rest of the fire crew from the pine flats all cried, howled, and carried on to see the feechiefriend leave. Tombro tried to give Aidan directions to the spot where they had left Aidan's backpack and civilizer clothes, but all his landmarks were stumps and fallen logs, which mostly look alike to a civilizer. Carpo and Pickro offered to pole him back as far as Scoggin Mound because, as Carpo put it, "We was the ones what brung you here." But Aidan was looking forward to a long boat journey with Dobro, his first and best feechie friend.

When Dobro poled off from the landing, a much-humbled Chief Larbo led the crowd in a farewell cheer: "Hee-haw for Pantherbane! His fights is our fights and our fights is his'n!"

Dobro and Aidan weren't alone in the flatboat. Benno Frogger was making the trip to the North Swamp too. He had decided to leave Larbo's band and rejoin Gergo's. It had been nearly two years since he had seen his mama, and he was in a hurry to get back to Bug Neck.

There had been so much to think about in the last day that Aidan had almost forgotten the last thing Maynard said before poling off into the southern reaches of the swamp. "Ask Dobro," he said, if Aidan wanted to know how Maynard had pulled off his scheme. How could Dobro have played a part in this? Aidan had to know what Maynard meant, and they weren't even out of sight of Bearhouse before he asked.

"Dobro, the false Wilderking—did you know he was my brother?"

"What?" Dobro asked incredulously, his face scrunched into a frown. Then a look of recognition dawned on his face. "Curly brown-headed feller? Looks a lot like you?"

Aidan nodded his head. His eyes narrowed. "How did you know that?"

Dobro sat down on the poling platform and let the push pole drag behind. His look of recognition was changing into a look of open-mouthed horror. "Did I . . . ?" he muttered. "Could I have . . . ?"

"When I asked my brother how he did it, how he tricked a whole band of feechies, he told me to ask you." Aidan's tone wasn't exactly accusatory, but neither was it the warmest Dobro had ever heard. "Did you meet my brother? What did you tell him?"

Dobro put fingertips to his temples, trying to think. "No," he said. "It couldn't have been . . ."

Aidan was getting impatient. "What happened?" he urged. His voice was a little louder. "Tell me what happened."

"I was coming up the river," Dobro began, "up near the meadow where you set with your sheep sometimes.

I looked through the trees, and I saw you setting under that big oak tree. Least I thought it was you. I decided I'd drop in on you."

Dobro thought for a minute, trying to get the details right. "No, wait a minute. It wasn't just me. Who was it with me?" He furrowed his brow in concentration. "Wait . . . It was you, weren't it, Benno?"

Benno turned around for the first time since Dobro started his story. "Huh? What'd you say? I weren't listening."

"I said you was with me the day I dropped in on Aidan's brother in the sheep meadow."

"Oh," Benno answered vaguely. "Now that you mention it, I do remember that."

"Anyway," Dobro continued, "we dropped out of the tree to howdy you, only it weren't you. It was your brother.

"And the peculiar thing," Dobro continued, "he wasn't surprised to see us. I mean, he was jumpified at first. I think we woke him up, if you want to know true. But it was almost like he was waiting for us to come. Ain't that right, Benno?" Benno gave a little grunt of agreement, but he had nothing to add.

"Well," continued Dobro, "we howdied him, and he howdied us back. And it weren't long before he commenced to asking us all kind of questions about feechie ways. Wanted to know about your feechiemark, Aidan, and what it meant. Wanted to know where we live and what kind of weapons we hunted with and did we know about the Wilderking and did we ever make war on other feechies."

Dobro shivered to recall it. "Made me feel uneasy in my mind. I know I ain't been the keerfullest feechie in the swamp when it comes to civilizers, but even I ain't gonna answer that kind of question."

"So what did you tell him?" pressed Aidan.

"Didn't tell him nothing," answered Dobro. "Just hemmed and hawed, and first chance we got to climb back up the tree, we took it."

"So you didn't give my brother anything that would help him trick Larbo's band?"

"Naw, Aidan. I promise. Cross my gizzard. Ask Benno."

Benno nodded his head. "Dobro told true. He didn't tell him nothing."

"And Benno didn't neither," added Dobro. "I can vouchify that."

Aidan's brow creased. He shook his head. "I don't understand," he murmured. "Maynard told me to ask my friend Dobro." Aidan tried to piece the whole thing together. How could Maynard have gotten a start on his scheme with no more than that to go on? How could Maynard have gone from that little bit of information— no information, really—to ruling a whole band of feechies as the Wilderking?

"*Awwww hawwwww hawwww hawwww!*" Benno burst into sudden, violent tears. "*Awwww hawwwww hawwww hawwww!* It was me what brought that rascal to the Feechiefen! It was me what brought such misery and heartache! *Awwww hawwwww hawwww hawwww!*"

Aidan and Dobro stared at Benno, astounded, as he continued to wail. "Slow down, Benno," Aidan coaxed. "What are you saying?"

"After me and Dobro was back in the woods," Benno sniffed, "I made out like I had somewhere else to be, and we parted ways. I circled around and found Maynard again."

"But why?" asked Dobro. His voice was full of hurt and betrayal.

"'Cause you had a civilizer friend and I wanted one too," bawled Benno. "'Cause you and the rest of the band thought I was a know-nothing show-off, but here was somebody wanted to listen to me talk."

Dobro looked down at his hands. It was true that he had never taken Benno very seriously. He had always waved off Benno's attempts to get attention and gain acceptance.

"So I told him everything he wanted to know," continued Benno, "and then some. I told him how I never got the say-so I deserved from my people, and he said he knew what that was like. I told him how I was figuring on going over to Larbo's band where I could get some respect, and he reckoned that wasn't a bad idea."

Benno reached into his side pouch and pulled out a steel hunting knife, identical to Aidan's. It had escaped the forge fires that morning. "And he give me this." Benno sighed as he watched the sun play on its burnished steel. "I knowed I had no business with a cold-shiny knife. But it shined as pretty as the sun on swamp water. And it made me feel special, you know, to be the only feechie in the band with a cold-shiny knife. Even if I never showed it to nobody, I liked to have it in my side pouch and know I was a little better than the folks around me, with their poor old stone knives.

"Every new moon, me and Maynard met in the sheep meadow, and he'd ask me questions about feechie ways. I felt just as smart and important as Chief Gergo hisself.

"Then one day Maynard asked me if I'd take him to meet Chief Larbo. I knowed that weren't a good idea. But I done it anyhow 'cause it made me feel important, you know, to say, 'Chief Larbo, let me introduce you to the man can outfit you with enough cold-shiny to whup this whole swamp.'"

Benno started crying again, loudly, sloppily. "I wanted to show you I was somebody, Dobro—you and everybody else in the band who treated me like a no'count bigtalker. I was mad at all of you. I just wanted to feel better." He wiped his eyes. "By the time it was over, I'd done ruint a whole band of feechies, and we weren't too far from ruining this whole swamp." He moaned like a wounded animal. "And I still didn't feel no better!"

He looked again at the hunting knife in his hand. The glint of the sun on its surface made little prisms through his tears. Then with a sudden, lurching movement he flung the knife into the deep blackness of the swamp. They watched the circles expand from the spot where the knife splashed down.

"Do you feel a little better now?" asked Dobro.

"Yeah," Benno answered. "A little better." A little smile softened his sorrow-crumpled face.

Aidan reached out to touch Benno's shoulder. "You're almost home now, Benno."

Chapter Twenty-three

The Last Leg

At Scoggin Mound, Benno left Dobro and Aidan to pole east toward Bug Neck. After a short visit with Aunt Seku and her grandchildren—which involved a snack of frog-egg jelly, much marveling over the frog orchid, and the happy return of Aidan's cold-shiny hunting knife—Aidan and Dobro poled on toward the scrub swamp at the northern edge of the Feechiefen. The travelers parted ways where the scrubby tanglewood lifted itself out of the black water. They bid one another good-bye with promises to meet again at the second full moon where the Bear Trail meets the River Trail, the spot where Dobro joined Aidan and Steren's boar hunt.

The scrub swamp was a challenge. Tree walking required two free hands, and one of Aidan's hands was occupied with the frog orchid. He managed at last to push through to the pine flats beyond. He didn't, however, find his backpack and civilizer clothes and so he had to cross the pine flats bare-chested, wearing his snakeskin kilt and turtle helmet. The pine forest, he was happy to find, was recovering nicely from the brushfire he and Hyko had started. In the two weeks since the fire, wire grass had already sprouted tender and green among the charred remains of its parent grass. All over the fire site, gopher tortoises munched on the fresh shoots.

When Aidan arrived at last at the broad river, he stood on the high bank and shouted toward Last Camp on the other side: "Massey! Floyd! Isom! Burl! Cooky!" Someone came to the bank on the civilizer side of the river. It was Isom, Aidan thought, but it was hard to tell so far away. Whoever it was, he didn't recognize Aidan, who jumped, waved, and yelled like a wild man. "It's me!" Aidan shouted. "Can you bring a boat?"

The river breeze carried Aidan's words downstream. All the hunter heard on the other side was incoherent hollering from what appeared to be a savage in a skirt and helmet. The hunter disappeared, and a dejected Aidan began preparing to swim one-handed across the wide, alligator-infested water.

But soon the hunter was back at the far bank, and he had several hunters with him. Aidan jumped around and wheeled his arms in a broad come-here gesture, but the men only stood in a knot, talking, obviously discussing what to do about the wild man on the other side of the river.

They were still talking when another man—tall and white-haired in a dusty tan robe—pushed past them and leaped into the nearest rowboat. When two goats jumped in after him, Aidan knew Bayard the Truthspeaker was pulling across the river to him.

"Bayard!" Aidan shouted when the old man nosed the rowboat into the root tangle at the river's edge. "What are you doing at Last Camp?"

"I heard about your fool's errand," the old prophet answered, "and I was headed into the Feechiefen to see if you needed rescuing. I was to leave Last Camp tomorrow morning."

Bayard looked at Aidan's outfit and laughed. "I'm not sure those boots go with that skirt," he remarked as he helped the young hero into the boat. Aidan situated the frog orchid at the boat's prow, where Bayard's goats would have to get past him to get to it. The poor flower was wilted and already brown around the edges, but it wasn't dead yet.

"So you found the frog orchid," the old man observed as he rowed the boat out of the eddy and into the open river.

"It found me, is more like it," said Aidan.

Bayard smiled. "Maybe. But I don't think the frog orchid could have found you, say, in Tambluff Castle or at your father's house or even at Last Camp." The prophet rowed in silence for a few pulls, then recited from the Frog Orchid Chant:

And in the orchid's essence pure
Is melancholy's surest cure.

Aidan looked at the sickly flower. "I don't know if the royal chemists will even be able to extract the essence out of this half-dead thing." He held the orchid out for Bayard to inspect. "Do you think they'll be able to, Bayard?"

Bayard didn't look at the plant. He looked into Aidan's eyes. "No, Aidan, they won't be able to. No chemist can extract the essence of a flower." He rowed a couple of pulls. "But you've experienced the frog orchid's essence."

Aidan smiled at the memory of Round Pond—that moment of peace that redeemed the turmoil of Bearhouse. Now he quoted the Frog Orchid Chant:

On oaken limb around a pond
As black as night, as round as sun.

"That's right," said Bayard. "How does a chemist extract that? The frog orchid does its healing work only on the adventurous soul who goes to it. Its essence can't be bottled and taken to one who will not make the journey."

Aidan fingered the drooping ribbons, which no longer looked like a frog's legs. "Aidan," Bayard said softly, "no chemist's art can heal what ails King Darrow."

Aidan fought back tears—tears of sadness and of anger too. "My king sent me to fetch him a frog orchid." He raised the broken oak limb from which the orchid sprouted. "I have fetched him a frog orchid, through many dangers and hardships." He wept openly now. "And I will bring it to Darrow's throne room. He is my king."

"That's right, Aidan," the prophet said soothingly. "That's right."

They were halfway across the river by now, and Little Haze, whose eyes were the sharpest among the hunters, recognized Aidan in the boat with Bayard. When the boat landed, the hunters of Last Camp lifted Aidan from the boat and carried him around the camp on their shoulders. Aidan still held the orchid in his hands to protect it from the goats.

Cooky was already roasting a wild boar on a spit. The hunters were having a special supper that night; it had been a whole week since the last nighttime attack on the camp, and they were celebrating.

But Aidan couldn't stay. He was too eager to get to Tambluff. A dead orchid wouldn't be a suitable offering for his king. He bathed in the river while the hunters gathered a new backpack for him and the few supplies he would need for the three-day hike up the Overland Trail and the River Road to Tambluff. Little Haze gave him a set of civilizer clothes, and Aidan and Bayard were off again.

The Overland Trail was like a pleasure stroll compared to the traveling Aidan had grown accustomed to. And being with the Truthspeaker sweetened the journey even more. "How did you learn of my quest for the frog orchid?" Aidan asked, fending off one of Bayard's goats, which was nibbling at the hem of his tunic.

"Your father told me." Bayard laughed at the look of surprise on Aidan's face. "He suspected you were heading into the Feechiefen. Then, about a week after you left, news trickled into Longleaf about the hunt feast and the way King Darrow sent you on your ridiculous mission."

"Was he worried? Father?"

"He took it surprisingly well," the old prophet answered. But Bayard grew pensive. "Your father's never been the same since Maynard died."

"Maynard's not dead." Aidan's words made the Truthspeaker stagger back a step, as if he had been struck a blow. Aidan told the story of the false Wilderking, from Maynard's encounter with Dobro and Benno in the bottom pasture to the Battle of Bearhouse and his poling away to the South Swamp. It is no easy thing to astonish a prophet, but Aidan astonished Bayard that day.

"It was a strange thing," said Aidan, "to look into my brother's eyes and see what he had become. It was like looking at what I might have become—who knows, at what I might become yet, if I don't guard my heart." Bayard nodded, listening, but he didn't say anything.

Aidan went on. "I know my brother is a liar and a fraud. But some of the things he said sounded right, made me wonder if I have what it takes to be the Wilderking." Aidan paused, collecting his thoughts. "He said that everything I ever had was given to me, that I haven't deserved any of it. I've been thinking about that. And I don't know. Maybe it's true."

Bayard threw back his head and laughed. "True? Of *course* it's true!"

Aidan was hoping for something more reassuring from the Truthspeaker. "What do you have that wasn't given to you?" the old man continued. "That's grace, man—what you're given, not what you deserve. And that's as true for Maynard as it is for you, as it is for me. Grace is the very air we breathe."

Aidan was still thinking about the things his brother had said to him. "Maynard said I didn't deserve to be the Wilderking any more than he did."

"Maybe. I don't know," Bayard answered. "Does a tall man deserve to be tall? Does Prince Steren deserve to be the son of a king? A bird might think he deserves to swim as well as a fish, but if he sits moping on the river-bank instead of using the wings God gave him, the fox is going to eat him.

"Your brother would rather have his own way than be happy. He's thrown away the grace he was given because it's not the grace he had in mind." The Truthspeaker paused to reflect on that. "There's not much hope for a person who won't live in the grace he's given."

‡ ‡ ‡

When the River Road brought the travelers to the gates of Longleaf Manor, they went their separate ways. Bayard insisted that he had to get to the hill country above Tambluff before dark. But there was another reason, a truer reason why the prophet wouldn't accompany Aidan to his father's house. Aidan had to face his father alone. It wasn't for Bayard to explain to Errol what had become of his second son. That was Aidan's task.

Moira, the cook, met Aidan in front of the manor house. "Aidan!" she called. "Welcome home!" She looked down at the orchid in Aidan's hands. "Your quest was successful, I see."

Aidan gave Moira a weary nod. Now that he was home again, he was starting to feel the exhaustion of his quest for the first time. Moira fingered the brown-edged orchid. "Looks like it has seen better days," she remarked. "I've grown orchids all my life. Why don't I see what I can do for this orchid while you go see your father. He'll be glad to see you safely home."

"Where is Father?" Aidan asked.

"You can find him in the cotton field," said Moira. "He's breaking in some new field hands." Aidan thought he detected a sly smile play about the corners of the cook's mouth. He handed the frog orchid to Moira and began the long walk to the cotton field. He still didn't know what he would tell Father about Maynard. His son's apparent death had crushed Errol. Would the news of Maynard's living be an even greater blow?

Father's back was turned when Aidan arrived at the cotton field. He had a heavy hoe and was vigorously chopping around cotton stalks while five slack-faced, surly field hands looked on. He was showing the proper method for hoeing a cotton field, and he looked as strong and healthy as Aidan had seen him in a long time. Errol motioned to his recruits to try for themselves. Their shaved heads bobbed up and down with their halfhearted effort; they looked more like storks than field hands. "Chop, men, chop!" Errol urged. "I'll make you farmers yet!"

Aidan sidled up alongside him. "Hello, Father," he said quietly. The old man turned to look at him. "Aidan!" he yelped with spontaneous joy. "Returned from the Feechiefen!" He took up his son in a bearish embrace. "My lost son is found!" he shouted. "Welcome, welcome, welcome home!" He called to the farmhands. "My boy Aidan! Home from the Feechiefen!" The farmhands gave him a sidelong look but didn't lift their heads from their work.

Errol broke into a little jig of excitement and relief. "So," he asked, his arm draped over Aidan's shoulder, "did you complete your quest? Did you find the frog orchid?"

"Yes, Father. Moira is tending to it now."

"I knew it!" Errol whooped. "I knew you'd come back with it!"

"I would have told you, Father," Aidan began, "but—"

Errol interrupted him. "Don't say another word about it."

Aidan was perplexed to see his father doing so well. This was the Father of old. Aidan hadn't seen him so energetic and chipper since before Maynard went away.

One of the farmhands straightened his back and pulled at his curling mustache. "Lorrrd Errrol," he said. "I think it's time to rrrest!"

"I'll say when it's time to rest," Errol answered sharply.

Aidan knew that voice, that curling mustache. These were the plume hunters he had met near Bullbat Bay. His eyes bulged in wonderment.

"You sent these boys just in time," Errol said. "With Jasper getting ready for the university and Brennus off at his own farm and you at Tambluff, I was in desperate need of help in the cotton field." He gestured at the plume hunters. "We burned their plume bale, but I thought they might like to have a chance to make some more respectable bales. They'll be here through the summer, then at harvest time we'll split the gold from whatever cotton bales we produce."

Aidan chuckled. "What makes you think these rascals will stay around till autumn?" he asked. But then he heard the clank of a heavy iron chain, and he realized that the five farmhands were shackled together.

"We got your pigeon note," Errol continued, "and when the plume hunters showed up with their plume bale the next day, we were ready for them. Your brothers and I and all the servants on the place threw them in chains." He smiled, remembering the scene. "Even Ebbe got in on the act."

Aidan looked at the two weeks' stubble on the five men's heads. "I didn't recognize them without their big hair."

"Well, I told them Tambluffer hairdos had no place on a working farm, not my working farm anyway." He nudged Aidan and whispered, "I plumed the plume hunters. I just can't find a hatmaker to buy the plumage." He slapped his knee, laughing at his own joke.

Aidan laughed, too, and shook his head. "It's going to be a long, hot summer for those mountain boys."

But every mention of the plume hunters stabbed at Aidan's conscience. He knew now, or thought he knew, the plume hunters were likely connected with Maynard. They were a reminder of the secret he was withholding from his father.

Father and son walked back to the manor house. Errol asked many questions about Aidan's journey into the swamp and back, but Aidan answered them evasively, studiously avoiding anything that would reveal any information about the false Wilderking. It just wasn't worth it, Aidan finally decided. Father was looking healthier, happier. Even in the three weeks since Aidan had seen him, Father seemed to have come to terms with the loss of Maynard. Why open that wound again? Maynard was better off dead. And Aidan was better off getting out of there until he was better prepared to talk to his father about what happened in Feechiefen.

"I've got to get back to Tambluff tonight," Aidan announced when they reached the manor house. "But I'll come back as soon as I can." Errol was understanding. He packed Aidan's supper himself and had his horse brought from the stable—the same horse Aidan had ridden down from Tambluff three weeks earlier. Moira's brief ministrations to the frog orchid had worked wonders. It wasn't exactly good as new, but it looked much more presentable.

Father followed Aidan out the door. On the front porch he asked the question he always asked anyone who came to Longleaf from the Eastern Wilderness: "Have you seen my son Maynard?"

Aidan froze. His eyes darted aside from his father's gaze as a lie formed in his mouth. He had decided he would never tell his father what he had seen on Bearhouse Island. But the lie wouldn't come out. His mouth wouldn't open.

Errol smiled at his son. "I know that Maynard lives," he whispered. "In the trial of the plume hunters, they told me who they worked for. They didn't even know

Maynard's real name. But I figured it out. I know what he's doing in the Feechiefen. I know he's impersonating the Wilderking. I know about his plot against King Darrow."

Errol looked beyond Aidan and down the cart path. "And it all breaks my heart." He paused. "But where there's life there's hope. And the heartache of knowing my son's wickedness is outweighed by the joy of knowing he's still alive and may yet turn back. I didn't have that hope when I thought he was dead."

Errol looked at Aidan's eyes now. "I can't explain it," he concluded, "except to say that I am still his father, and he is still my son."

Chapter Twenty-four

Throne Room

King Darrow could hear his son's exuberant shouts even before he burst uninvited into the throne room. "Father! Father! He's back! Aidan has returned from the Feechiefen!"

The castle was already buzzing with the news. Even in the city of Tambluff, the rumor was starting to spread that Aidan Errolson had gone into the Feechiefen and come out again bearing the frog orchid of old lore.

The king was in a darker mood than usual that night. His melancholic episodes had grown noticeably meaner and more frequent in the three weeks or so since the hunt feast. That night he sat sulking in the glum light of torches, refusing to let his servants light the brighter-burning wax candles.

Steren's voice echoed against the sandstone walls. "Father! Our prayers are answered! The frog orchid is here and Aidan is alive! Your melancholy is cured!"

The king cast heavy-lidded eyes on Steren. He neither smiled nor gave any other signal he had heard or even recognized his son.

"Should I bring him in?" asked Steren eagerly. "Do you want to see the frog orchid?" King Darrow didn't speak but waved a hand in an ambiguous gesture. He might have been granting Steren permission or he might have been shooing him away. Steren took it as a gesture of permission and darted out of the room to fetch Aidan. He came back immediately, pulling the returning hero by the arm. In his hands Aidan held a tree branch, and above it, on a long, limber stem, nodded a delicate white flower trailing two long ribbons like the springy legs of a leaping frog.

At the very sight of the frog orchid, Darrow felt his spirits lift. A man would have to be made of stone not to be affected by a thing of such exquisite beauty. Perhaps it was, as the old lore said, "melancholy's surest cure."

Aidan knelt before the king's throne. Bowing deeply, he held the flower out as an offering to the king. "Your Majesty," he said, "the frog orchid. Out of many perils and many hardships, I bring this gift to you."

Darrow took the branch and flower from the kneeling Aidan. He turned the branch around in his hands and examined the flower's delicate beauty from every angle. A smile softened his face, the first smile Steren had seen in days. The true King Darrow seemed to be breaking through the cloud of melancholy that had obscured him these many months. It wasn't just the flower itself that touched the king, but the sacrifice of this boy, a boy he had believed to be his enemy, in the service of his king. Even as his smile of happiness grew, a tear of regret began to form in the king's eye. He silently vowed to be more worthy of such loyalty.

The king rose and carried the flower to a torch, to see it better in the light. But as he stood in the torchlight, the jealousy and hatred that had caused him to send Aidan to the Feechiefen in the first place washed over him again like a wave. With a sudden movement he snapped the flower from its stem and dangled it over the licking flames of the torch. The long, ribbony legs of the frog orchid shriveled in the blaze. Then the king plucked the petals one by one and watched them curl and smoke as he dropped them into the fire. Then he dropped the bud, the last morsel of the flower, into the torch.

Darrow turned and spoke to Aidan for the first time but without emotion: "There is only one way the frog orchid could have cured my melancholy: only if it had lured you to your death in the Feechiefen Swamp."

Aidan's eyes filled with tears. He realized that his king was lost and that he could do nothing to bring him back. There wasn't much hope, as the prophet had said, for a man who wouldn't live in the grace he was given. The Truthspeaker had warned him: No chemist could cure what ailed King Darrow. And yet, Aidan hadn't believed it until he saw the look of hatred in the king's eyes. Aidan turned and ran from the throne room. At last he understood that his days in King Darrow's court were over.

EXPERIENCE WHERE IT ALL BEGAN!

The Bark of the Bog Owl

Book One: The Wilderking Series by Jonathan Rogers

"…a new level in imaginative fantasy…faith fiction readers of
all ages should enjoy this first installment in the trilogy."

–Publishers Weekly

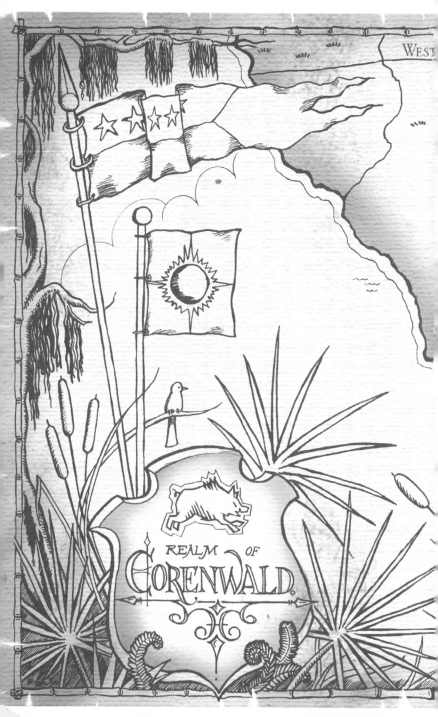

WEST

REALM — OF —

GORENWALD